I0571766

Queen &
Commander

Book One of the Hive Queen Saga

Janine A. Southard

Cover by MaeIDesign and Photography
Editing by Cat Rambo
Copyediting by Rachel Solomon

ISBN: 978-0-9886468-5-8

Winning a ship means surpassing the competition.

The three competing Queens swiveled their heads, hare-quick, to home in on new prey. They'd ignored her until she'd made that noise. Now they had the scent of fresh insecurity and would peck away until they laid her meager confidence bare for the massacre.

"What a sweet little girl," gushed the one in red. "Where's your mother?"

Dead, actually. Well, if this Queen planned to come after her for her age, she'd show her appreciation in the way only a younger person could. She raised her eyebrows and furrowed them down the middle, then pulled her head back onto her neck as though repulsed or doing a proper sit-up.

From the way the older woman cringed back, Rhiannon knew she'd succeeded in making the derisive *Did you seriously just say that to me?* face that she'd seen on her more critical peers.

A teenager can out bitch-face you any time, Queenie. Don't try that tactic with me.

The eldest cocked her head, more curious than cruel. Perhaps she found it as difficult to gauge Rhiannon's age as the other way around. As far as Rhiannon knew, this woman had been one of Dyfed's first Queens, self-made and just as untrained as herself. "Why do you think you deserve *Ceridwen's Cauldron*?"

Acknowledgements

Gigantic thanks go out to my Kickstarter backers. Without your support, *Queen & Commander* would not be the book it is today. Thank you for believing in this novel and for sharing my passion for ensemble space opera. In particular, I'd like to thank the following backers for their contributions (in alphabetical order by first name because you have to order things somehow):

Amit Wadhwa
Andrea Scardina
Anna Box
Brysen Bristow
Chad Nedzlek
Charles P. Howerton
Chris Battey
Claire Rousseau
Dominic Bell
Gurashish S Brar
Heather Hintze
James Truher
Jay & Dolores Southard
Jay Groven
Jeffrey Krauss
Jenny Yang
Jess Haley

Johanna

Jon Foulds

K. Crouch

Kruegers

Lisa Bloch

Mark Kadas

Melissa Louie

Melissa Pagonis

Miriah Hetherington

Olivia Johnson

Scott & Sandra Kurtzeborn

Stevie Carroll

Ted W. Way

Trevor Harris

And, of course, special thanks to Jeremy Barton, my "main investor" and spouse.

Chapter One

Trial by Multiple Choice

For months, Rhiannon hunched over borrowed old exams while her friends danced and sang outdoors. Her nights were consumed with studying. This day, Test Day, she'd learn whether all that effort could lead to the future she wanted. Not the future society wanted for her.

She stood in silence on the well-swept stone floor outside the classroom. The stitched ash tree on her uniform shirt scraped against her skin. What was the point of wearing it anyway, hidden beneath impractical, white formal robes?

At the head of the line, a boy palmed in under the proctor's watchful eye. He collected his blue pad—embossed with the same ash tree symbol, officially encrypted—and entered the Test room.

Everyone shuffled forward a space. Rhiannon among them.

Soon enough, though, she'd be admitted. Soon enough, she'd read the familiar questions. Soon enough, she could change out of this formal wear.

They said it was impossible to study for the Test. Oh, you could study facts and figures. You could study poets and history. But you couldn't study yourself into being an extrovert or into analytical inclinations. You couldn't cheat all of society. And if you tried, you'd be found out. Or, at least, *very* unhappy in your unsuited life.

Rhiannon had studied.

When she was nine and her mother had died, she'd studied heart conditions; she'd studied doctors' expressions as they swore it wasn't her fault. When the other students in third form enthused over competitive choir, she'd studied the usual things—math, biology, poetry—but so ferociously that no one noticed her lack of choral talent. When Gwyn's attention turned more to horticulture than her best friend, Rhiannon had studied plant genera and topiaries in order to follow her into this new territory.

This year, her final school year, she'd studied for the Test.

She looked beyond the proctor who guarded the door, checking whether she'd have a friend inside. Even if it was forbidden to talk in the Test room, she'd still prefer to sit beside Gwyn—or even Victor—than some stranger from the other side of town. She didn't want to be alone.

The kid in front of her palmed in, collected his blue pad, and joined the other sixteen-year-olds, cutting her seeking short. The odd cough or bootscrape on vomit-yellow carpet surprised the hush of the room beyond.

Her turn. Rhiannon pressed her skin to the sticky, warm identification plate.

Beep. Beep. Beep.

The proctor turned his pad to face her. It flashed a message: *Report to room 203. / Cer i'r ystafell 203.*

Her jaw resonated, hollow, with her measured breaths.

I'm not in trouble. Students get sent to new rooms all the time during standardized testing. Plenty of people might get reshuffled on Test day.

No one could possibly suspect her illicit studying. Everyone knew that life's happiness flowed from honest answers. Ever since the first Test 120 years ago. One hundred twenty years in *mlynedd Cymraeg,* just over 135 Earth years.

She spared the room one more look. Gwyn sat near the window, somehow elegant in the too-small desk, twisting her near-white hair around a finger.

Rhiannon adored Gwyn's snowy hair. She'd nicknamed her for it on the day they met. In a way, the name was Rhiannon's mark, transforming Gwyn from *random kid* into *Rhiannon's friend* as far as their teachers were concerned.

Gwyn beckoned her over, but Rhiannon shook her head. She had somewhere else to be, it seemed.

Everything was fine. She'd find room 203 and take the Test as planned. She'd prepared for this. Nothing could go wrong.

She flew through the halls, a mere fifteen minutes early now and unlikely to merit a good seat in this new room. The closer she got to the elevator, the fewer people she saw. She'd left the crowds of vibrating students behind. Oppressive emptiness rose up to swallow and mute the distant chatter.

She slowed her steps, double-checked the signs. No, the elevator hadn't moved in the last day.

The clicking from her boot heels bounced off the lockers like a metronome. She found herself counting out the musical timing. Measures of four-four, two beats for each click. *One, TWO, three, FOUR.* If she trusted her voice, she could break into song.

She didn't.

She continued counting as she rode the boxy elevator—free of sticky candy or torn papers on this auspicious day—to the second floor.

A floor she'd have sworn was closed off for teacher in-service during the Test.

The second floor matched the first. The same stone-tiled floor in the hallways, the same locker banks along the wall. But it was smaller, only five doorways long, and the interior carpets were pea-soup green. Walking the near-deserted hall was like walking into Annwyn's Otherworld, another dimension just slightly different from their own.

Not that she believed in Annwyn or Arawn or Manawyddan. She danced in the groves on holy days, like her Mom used to insist, but that was it.

Four students waited in a loose queue in the stunted hall. No proctor stood before the door to bar the way. Rhiannon recognized three from her specialized placement classes in statistical analysis, legal analysis, and computational methods. They'd placed at the tops of those sections, though she'd never seen them in her poetry or theatre classes.

She didn't know the fourth. Probably an analytical prodigy from a different school, taking the Test here for administrative reasons.

Rhiannon fell into her place at the queue's end and joined the others in watching the closed door. This was it. She wasn't even going to get to take the Test. She'd already been typecast as a Perceiver, and Dyfed needed all the Perceivers it could get. Needed anyone who could consistently predict the future's needs, a rare talent. A Perceiver made sure important issues worked out right. The first time. Economic systems and defense strategies didn't get do-overs.

All that studying! All that learning how best to answer *Do you feel more energetic after attending a party or spending time alone?* All that courage-sticking to dumb down her analytic answers, lest her Perceiver skills overwhelm her desired results.

All that belief that she could choose her own future...

Sniffling behind her made her turn. A sweaty, blonde boy had joined the end of the queue. He rubbed at his nose, pulled at his hair, and sidled from one foot to the other.

Nervous Ned? She gifted him with a polite smile before turning back to the door. *What's Ned doing here?*

Rhiannon pushed her wavy, near-black hair back from her face, relieved when cooler air touched overheated skin. Ned didn't have any Perceiver tendencies, except when it came to rocks. He hoped to become a Geologist, she knew. Sure, he'd learned the same analytic principles as the rest of the students in line, but he only used them for Geology. He didn't have the obsessive-intuitive tendencies of a student who'd aced three cross-disciplinary analysis sections.

His presence broke her model.

One by one, the four students ahead of her went into the Test room. One by one, they emerged a few minutes later, shaking and smiling. One by one, they disappeared into the elevator.

The Test was a full-day event. They certainly hadn't taken it. So what had they done in that closed room? Her turn to enter the room. It was claustrophobic. Antique *physical* books crammed into wall shelves, more piled on the floor. Someone had tried to brighten the windowless chamber with wrinkled flags from all Dyfed's cities. Three-by-three, the flags overlapped the books.

A tenth flag dwarfed the local standards. It came from Earth. The real Welsh one with the red dragon. Under it, two adults sat at long, steel desks that teetered with stacks of papers. She'd never seen either of them at the school before. They had to be from some State office, probably the Senedd.

The man further back gestured to the chair at his desk.

He was decently old for someone who must be an official Test Administrator, maybe 90 or 100, with gray-streaked hair and a wrinkled jacket over his tunic. He had a severe hooked nose, tempered by surrounding lines that alluded to frequent smiles. Rhiannon decided he was the *helpful but powerless* type. If she asked him the right questions, she could harvest clusters of data.

"You're not in trouble," he began as she sat down.

She'd figured as much without his help, but nodded to encourage him to continue.

"In fact, you're one of the lucky few who don't have to wait until tomorrow to find out what the future holds."

She painted a smile on her face, refusing to let her head fall forward. She'd tested out of the Test. *Perceiver status and lifelong boredom, here I come.* Hands clenched in her lap, she leaned towards him as if interested in hearing him pronounce her life sentence.

"A small percentage of students worry about their Test results each year, so much so that they over-practice. Point oh three six percent, actually." His hands danced, shaping figures in the air, oblivious to her hidden disinterest. "You're in an even smaller population. See, ninety-two percent of those students turn out to be Perceivers, or at least very high-level Analysts. But that remaining eight percent are really just nervous types who can belong to any skill and interest class."

Her eyes flicked up to meet the administrator's as he smiled at her. If she classed as one of the nervous eight

13

percent, then what did he think she was? *O patient Man-awyddan, please don't let all that studying be in vain.* She still had a chance. She'd Tested consistently on her last twenty practice exams.

She wanted to be a Queen. Not because of the societal power. Not because it meant the boys would fawn over her like they did in films. But because she wanted to be with people. She wanted to build a family, a family she could trust. A family that would never leave. She loved her father and her best friend, but they were only two people in all the universe. A Queen had more. A Queen had perfect love and Devotion. A Queen had her choice of the male top tenth of a percent. And those men flocked to her banner.

If you don't think I'm a Perceiver, Test Administrator, do my Test results tell you I'm a Queen?

"Now, you're interesting, because your first practice results show strong Perceiver abilities." He shook his head. "But no! That was one of your nervous Tests. You are a very lucky young lady. If that had been your real Test result, well..."

She breathed faster, willing him to speed up with her.

"Your subsequent practice results, though—did you know that you've answered *every* Test question three times over?—are split between Queen and Queen-Commander. Your third highest category was still Analyst, which might explain why our statistics are off this year." He ducked forward conspiratorially. "If you'd actually been a Perceiver, we'd have held onto that ninety two per-cent Perceiver number, but..."

He trailed off, letting her fill in the blank. She did the math, looking off into the air behind his right shoulder as she visualized the numbers on each side of the equality symbol in order for there to be $.92x = y$ where y is the number of students exempted.

"But don't worry!" The administrator pulled her attention back to the conversation as he hastened to reassure her. "The university we've picked for you has a ninety-five percent counseling success rate in working that nerv-ousness out. And even the remaining five percent still make tidy Queens, though not Commanders, in a variety of fields. Your scores aren't career-limiting."

He rambled on about her required counseling regime, cautioning her she couldn't tell anyone about this way to avoid the Test.

But she ceased to listen. She'd made it. She'd Tested as a Queen and Commander.

She thought of Earth's great Queens: Hatshepsut, Elizabeth, Victoria. *And now Rhiannon.* She looked down at her hands shaking in her lap and admitted it to herself: she might be the slightest bit giddy.

Lucky Rhiannon, born on a world with Tests to fool and Queens to become.

Test after practice Test, she'd reworked her answers to *What are your favorite activities?* paired against different values for *What is the difference between a theory and a hypothesis?* Only last week, she'd consistently massaged her results to either Queen or Commander.

She should go home. But what would she do when she got there? She'd finished studying. She'd studied her way into a future *she'd* picked. She shouldn't have been able to, but she'd done it.

Now what?

A slow smile pulled at her lips as she shook the administrator's hand. In a daze, she waved Nervous Ned in for his turn. She'd won. She'd gotten the future she chose, not the one the Test would have predicted. She'd beaten the Test.

Manawyddan's mousetrap! If she could do that, then she could do anything.

Her new status tasted like victory.

CHAPTER TWO

Skill-crossed Lovers

The moment he'd finished the Test, Victor hopped on his so-old-it's-rusting bike and raced to the park to meet his secret girlfriend.

He knew how he'd Tested. *Intelligence in the top half-percent. Skilled with computers. Creative. Predisposed to fixate on one worthy woman.* The Test result he'd dreamed of since childhood. But that was before he'd met Gwyn.

Gods, Victor thought, *I'm destined to be unhappy.*

Tomorrow, the Senedd would tell him what he already knew. They'd provide all the best training. They'd make him a CreaTech who would one day Devote himself to the most brilliant and beautiful of Queens.

They'd send him away from here. Never to see Gwyn again. He choked on the melancholy.

He had to take advantage of this last chance to be together. She already knelt beneath *their* tree. Silent. Peaceful.

He dropped down beside her and rested his head resting in his girlfriend's lap. He could only call her his girlfriend for a little longer before he'd have to find someone else. Someone society approved of. Someone who'd Tested as a Queen.

He stared into the canopy of five-pointed silver maple leaves above them while she soothed his hair. *Will there even be trees wherever they send me?*

He closed his eyes against the occluded sun and the veined leaves and the white-blonde hair that obscured his Gwyn's face. He couldn't look at his perfect world right now. Couldn't bear to witness everything he'd be missing.

He wanted to be a CreaTech, to Devote. Of course he did! Who wouldn't want to join the rarefied top classes of intelligentsia and happiness? But not at this price. Not if he had to lose this beautiful girl who knew everything about animals and cried for him whenever his father left on a long trip without saying goodbye.

Victor dug his fingers hard into the green grass, determined to drive them in so deeply that they'd strike rock. He wanted to bleed, to scream his agony. The pain would make more sense than this slow death in his heart.

Water fell down onto his forehead. *Gwyn.* He wrested dirt-crusted fingers from the ground and brushed them against her pale cheeks, smearing her perfect face with brown mud. Even in their shared pain, looking at her made his mouth tremble upwards and his lungs expand.

"Shh, shhh."

He sat up to wrap Gwyn in his arms, chancing a brief hug. Their love had been hidden away from the world for the last two years, like water at the bottom of a core-deep well.

"We can find a way to be together. If not now, maybe in twenty years. I'll be old enough then to have contact with women outside my Hive."

She clutched at his shirt. Victor gave up on speaking. He rested his head on her silken hair, rubbing it with his cheek. It wasn't fair! Why couldn't Gwyn be a Queen? Why couldn't he have both a Queen and a love? Gods knew his own often-absent father tried to have both. *Though Dad spends more time with his Queen than with us.*

She pushed back from him. Their eyes met, dull brown to greening hazel. Her nose scrunched, reddening already.

He had to make this better somehow. Victor leaned forward and slanted his mouth across hers. He wanted to fix things, to make her concentrate on the good they still had left. He wanted to eat her sadness until none remained.

Pressed against her, surrounded by tender sorrow, Victor didn't notice the interloper until it was too late.

A throat cleared behind him. They'd been found out. His new university would be warned. They'd be told that he was *defective*, previously involved with a non-Queen. They'd whisper about him in the university halls. They'd never let him see Gwyn again, not even twenty years from now.

Victor's anxious eyes flitted past grey scaly tree bark. Past his bicycle's front wheel, tilted at a useless angle. To the newcomer's heeled boots, graduating into crimson silk harem pants. That style was not at all fashionable in Dyfed's cities and towns. In fact, he only knew one person who'd wear such clothing.

A strangled breath rushed from him, falling harmlessly to the ground.

Victor pulled Gwyn tighter against his side. Her cool peacefulness stabilized him. "Hey, Gav."

"We survived!" Gavin crowed. He held out a hand, palm facing down, for a celebratory handshake. When Victor didn't reciprocate, the hand fell back to Gavin's bulky-trousered side. "Ooookay." Gavin drew out the word in friendly mockery and flopped onto the grass beside them.

The contented bastard.

Gavin looked up into the grey-blue sky to point towards a shiny cloud cluster where the spaceport orbited. "There's a new ship in at the spaceport," he said, apropos of nothing.

Just what I need, another anywhere-but-here rant about leaving our planet behind. "What's this one?" Victor asked. He wished his friend would go away and leave him and Gwyn to mourn their imminent sundering.

Gavin popped a Tribute in his mouth. Victor and Gwyn both declined the package he offered.

"The *Ceridwen's Cauldron*. She's an in-system hauler right now, but she's about to change her complement completely. I hear she's being put into the Hive-training system. Only needs a Queen and five Devoted crewmembers. Wish I was one. What I wouldn't give to get away from Dyfed! I'd even be a toilet scrubber to get out of this crazy place. What was Mom thinking when she brought me here?"

He struck a pose. "Was she thinking my face was old and tired? I wasn't normal, but I was happy," he declaimed. Gavin's mom was a renowned and well-traveled actress, so Gavin's schooling came from plays and foreigners. It showed whenever he quoted supposedly famous plays that no one else had ever heard of. *I don't know what that's supposed to mean, Gav.*

Victor's heart had finally slowed to its original steady pace. He'd been half-relieved to get caught with his beloved. It made him wonder. Maybe he should do what his dad didn't. Maybe he should skip going to university, skip finding a suitable Queen. Maybe he should bow to his Devoted nature, should give himself to his true love. He could hunt for a Queen later. If any still wanted him.

But to do that, he and his love—his Gwyn—needed to escape Dyfed. Needed to get away from the society whose life-planning linked the brightest male minds with a brilliantly charismatic female. Young Hives depended on their members' romantic love for a Queen. It unified them. But at the price of outside relationships. Victor didn't want to be like his dad, who split his love between his family and a woman Victor had met only once. He didn't want to feel this way about anyone other than Gwyn.

What choice did he have? But Gavin had roused an idea... They could go somewhere far away from here in the *Ceridwen's Cauldron*, could come back when they were old enough to raise no questions of propriety. Gavin knew all about off-planet living. Even though his mom was Dyfed-raised, he'd only moved back this year.

If the ship needed a Hive crew and captain, all they needed was a Queen-captain who would accept them all.

"Did you know?" Victor said. Casual as mentioning a tree's growth. "Rhiannon Tested as Queen and Commander this morning." Scores weren't supposed to be released till the next day at school, but the pathetic security guarding them was made to be bypassed. He'd checked all his friends' results.

Gwyn straightened from her cuddled position against his side.

"She did?" she asked, incredulous. "Good for her." She settled against him again with a sigh. "I'm glad one of us got everything she wanted."

They weren't getting it.

Victor tried again. "So if she's a Queen, she and her Hive qualify for the *Cauldron*. We three make most of the crew, even if Gwyn can't technically Devote. We'd just need two more to fit the ship's requirements." He gripped Gwyn's shoulders tightly. *Rhiannon's the perfect solution. She won't try to steal my love away from her best friend.* "We could do this. We could stay together."

Gavin stood, his blue eyes focused on the sky-speck above. "Far away from here, in a better place." His shoulders hunched forward. "I wouldn't *really* have to Devote to your friend, would I? This whole stupid planet with its stupid Devoted Hives and stupid expectation of everlasting obsession makes me sick."

Victor shook his head, dark brown hair flopping into his eyes. *You don't even know Rhiannon yet. You might end up loving her as a Devoted should. What are you worried about?* "We'll pretend. I mean, Gwyn's a girl and can't Devote at all, and I'm not sure about splitting myself between two women. But it'll work. We can pay lip-service to Devotion and still get everything."

This time when Gavin held out a hand to perform a victory handshake, Victor let himself be pulled into the motions. Even the cheek kiss and hop in a circle. When he tried to get Gwyn to try it as well, though, she moved away.

"Hey, no." He reached for her again, but she danced backwards. "What's wrong, sweetheart?" He caught her delicate wrist in the noose of his thumb and middle finger.

Her face was cautious. "We don't know that Rhi will even go for this. I don't want to ruin her life. She made *Queen* and *Commander*. Do you know what that must mean for her?"

Victor didn't care what it meant for *her*. He just knew what it meant for *them*. Rhiannon was their ticket to freedom and the perfect life. "Of course she'll go for it if *you* ask her. Call her, right now. Ask her to meet us here. The worst she can say is no."

He'd never seen Rhiannon deny Gwyn anything. Two years ago, he'd wondered if he even had a chance with the shy, sweet Gwyn or if the girls were dating each other.

Gwyn thrust her hands into pockets too small for her long fingers. But after a bit more wheedling, she pulled out her pad and flashed the message to Rhiannon.

The new Queenlet would never know what hit her.

CHAPTER THREE

Center of My Universe

By late afternoon on Test Day, the wide streets were still mostly empty. Whistling breezes echoed in the middle of civilization, usually unheard outside the groves.

Everyone had stayed home that day—work stopped, play stopped, drinking stopped—to make sure that the Test could be administered free of distraction. The only people out in the dimming red light now were the truly stressed and the happily aimless, flitting to their new destinations on their own time.

Rhiannon fell into the flitting category. She approached the park, still dazed from the morning's happy outcome. She closed her eyes to better bask in the sunlight bathing her face. Its happy warmth reminded her of times with her mother.

A tear cooled her cheek at the thought. Rhiannon took pride that it was only one.

Up ahead, three figures sat beneath the tree she'd marked as *Gwyn's*. She waved an arm over her head, and the large motion filled her with extra adrenaline. She jogged the rest of the way. Twigs crunched beneath her polished boots as she closed with them.

She couldn't wait to tell Gwyn all about making Queen and Commander. The administrator had said something about not telling anyone that enough pre-Testing made actual Testing irrelevant. So, fine, she could skip that part. But the part about getting out of Perceivership and into Queen training? She was bursting to share that with her best friend, her only friend since Mom died.

Her smile faded as she recognized Victor in the little coterie. While Rhiannon had gotten what she wanted on the Test, Gwyn hadn't gotten everything. Gwyn would be forced away from Victor.

Victor pounced upon her the moment she drew close enough. "You want Gwyn to be happy, right?"

Oh, this can't be good. Of course she wanted Gwyn to be happy. No one meant more to her than Gwyn. Gwyn, who had become Rhiannon's sun and water during the hard years after her mother's death. Gwyn, who had offered unconditional friendship when Rhiannon had forgotten how to interact with other children. Gwyn, who had never given up during Rhiannon's awkward phase.

Yes, Rhiannon wanted Gwyn to be happy. But she wasn't sure that Victor wanted *Rhiannon* to be happy.

Well, on one score, she and Victor agreed: Gwyn came first.

She ignored the question. "Hello, Victor." She passed him to hug her best friend. She extended a hand to the third party member— a runner-thin, flamboyant dresser. "Hi, I'm Rhiannon."

The boy had reddish blonde hair, a mischievous grin, and an exceedingly thin nose surrounded by an outdoor-person's freckles. He scrambled to his feet and took that hand, bending over it like a Shakespearean actor. "Gavin. It's an honor to meet you." He looked up at her through playful eyelashes, still bent over her hand. "My lady."

What a ham! But a delightful ham. Not that she could do anything about it for another few decades. Queenship's downside: no relationships that might damage your Hive's dynamic.

Someday, though. Someday, she'd meet someone she truly loved, and her Hive would allow her to pursue that someone.

In her peripheral vision, graceful Gwyn stumbled forward to get her attention.

"We, well Victor wanted me to ask... That is, he thinks we could..." Gwyn gave up, and Rhiannon wished she could protect the other girl from whatever had upset her so.

"What Gwyn's trying to say." Victor stepped forward to speak for Gwyn. That brassed Rhiannon. Sure, the girl was wobbling into her explanations, but that was no reason to cut her off. *Ugh.* Then again, Rhiannon had been known to take over in high-anxiety situations, so maybe it wasn't so bad. "She's trying to ask you to join us."

27

"Join you?"

"Join our Hive. As our Queen."

She blanked her face into the *unamused* non-expression. That made as close to no sense as made no difference. You couldn't ask a Queen to join a Hive. That was backwards. If you were lucky, maybe she asked you. Otherwise, you *begged* to join her. But the other way around?

The Shakespearean ham in the overwhelmingly voluminous clothes tried to salvage the conversation. Clearly he at least understood what her tightening eyebrows meant.

"We were talking about starting an Explorer Hive," he explained deferentially, "and Victor said we couldn't do it with any Queen but you."

I'll just bet. No other Queen would accept him and Gwyn. On the one ash branch, it sounded ideal. A ready-made Hive that needed her to step in. But on the other branch... "I haven't been trained." *Bran's blood! I earned that training. Even the laughable nervousness counseling.*

She needed that training too. She'd be the first to admit that she had no idea how to be charismatic, half a Queen's job. And she couldn't even identify the other half!

Not to mention she wanted the Commander classes. She wanted to learn personnel organization, much made of in military film. She wanted to be with people. To be a part of the world, not locked away and buried under soulless data.

Gavin shrugged slender shoulders, displaying impressive muscles in the process. "I'm sure you can read all about it. And we'd be there to help you with the exercises in any textbooks you bring."

It *was* true that she could study on her own. She'd never needed to physically attend a class before, and those first Queens had found their own ways. But still. "I got into New Cardiff, you know. A degree from there, the potential Devotees I'd connect with... I hate to lose those. Can't this plan wait a few years? I'll still happily take you."

Victor buried his head in his hands, a good copy of her own favorite posture for communicating frustration. She found it hard to take seriously.

Gavin pointed skyward, his many sleeves inching up towards his head. "Ah, but in a few years there won't be a ship at the spaceport ripe for the picking."

The sun and the terrible metaphor momentarily blinded her. "Come again?"

Gavin explained. He explained about the ship, *Ceridwen's Cauldron*, with its beautiful, alliterative name. He explained that this was the perfect opportunity to provide for the skill-crossed lovers *and* to get practical experience. He explained that this chance might not come again for decades. He explained his general dissatisfaction with the Devotion system, but that he'd been struck by her sensibility and was happy to join her Hive if she'd have him.

He didn't explain that their whole ridiculous plan hinged on her.

But she understood it anyway. Without her, Gwyn couldn't go with Victor. Without her, Victor would grow into a man who considered today's foibles a youthful dalliance. Without her, Gavin... Well, she wasn't sure about Gavin yet.

The point was, without her, their plan crumbled. With her, her own plans crumbled. She'd never be able to come back. If she left, she forfeited her place at New Cardiff. She'd be labeled an unreliable Queen. The Senedd *might* try to rehabilitate a damaged Queen, with Queens in such demand, but it wasn't the way she'd bet.

Gwyn pushed past the boys, her white-blonde hair shimmering in the early-evening sunlight. She stooped to equalize their heights and tangled her long, garden-rough fingers with Rhiannon's.

"Please." Gwyn whispered it first, then repeated it more loudly. "Please, Rhi. Don't send me away."

Away from Victor or away from Rhiannon? It didn't matter. She couldn't deny the quiet plea. "Anything for you, love. You know you can count on me."

That was the end of that. No use dwelling on what she couldn't change.

Fingers still grasping Gwyn's chapped skin, she addressed Gavin, who seemed the most knowledgeable in these matters. "What will we need?"

"Six crew, including the Queen-captain, and an application form," he answered promptly. "I have one right here."

She bit back a laugh at his preparedness. Perhaps Victor and Gwyn only just concocted this scheme, but the new guy had seen the light long ago. "Since you're so keen," she said, tilting her head to keep the words from seeming too serious, "you can fill out all the essays."

She could always revise whatever he wrote. Plus, it wasn't like she had plans for the ship yet. Reading his compositions would give her more information about his style and intentions. Maybe she'd get lucky and he'd be a terrible writer.

He raised a hand to his ear without actually tucking any hair behind it. His cheeks puffed into circles. "I'm honored that you trust me with such a task."

She refused to feel guilty over hoping for unsalvageable essays. Either they'd get the ship, thanks to his solid work. Or their application would be rejected and it wouldn't be Rhiannon's fault.

That part delegated, she still needed to find two more crew for her faux-Hive. She wouldn't let Victor get them for her. He already had more control over this scheme than she did, no matter who bore which title. No, she had an idea for their merry band's next member. She probably shouldn't involve him, but she was sure that Luciano would follow her anywhere.

Even if he shouldn't.

She'd destroy him, she knew. She'd pull him away from his well-planned future, the future he'd moved to Dyfed to pursue. But that wouldn't stop her.

She'd destroy him for Gwyn.

31

CHAPTER FOUR

For the Right Queen

The day after the Test, no teachers expected their sixteen-year-old students to pay attention. God knew that Luciano tried, but he'd spent most periods thinking about his spectacular good fortune. He'd Tested as Devoted and Medical Doctor. The Senedd would pay for his education!

He drafted a million letters home in his head. His mother and sister on the mining colony Nuova would be so proud. They'd also be pleased they'd enjoy a greater portion of his paychecks, once the Senedd started sponsoring his tuition and board at the University of Dyfed.

Rhiannon came up beside him after his last class. Her matte red tunic made her dark locks shine.

"Hi, Luciano," she said.

That was something he'd adored about Rhiannon since he'd met her. She always said his full name. She never called him Luke or Lucky, like the construction crew at his off-campus job. She never assumed his Italian-miner accent made him an idiot.

When the Test results had gone up, he'd checked her name in the lists. He'd worried that she'd grow apart from him and start spending time with the vapid Queenlets who sat in front of the vending machines and demanded favors to let anyone pass. Yet here she was, initiating conversation.

"I saw you made Queen and Commander," he said.

"And you got Devoted and Medical."

She'd noticed his scores and remembered them? He hadn't realized she cared enough to look him up. He was just the new guy. She had local friends, childhood friends, but she'd searched out *his* name. It couldn't have been easy. *Luciano Totti* was on a far different reporting board than *Rhiannon Jones*, separated by sex and alphabet.

He shoved trembling fingers into his pockets. Here was proof she wanted to be friends. Maybe, before she'd become Queen, she'd even wanted more than friendship.

"Yeah," he said.

Outside the school, adults and children alike pushed and weaved their ways down busy sidewalks. The sweaty overcrowding almost overwhelmed the sugary tang of safety-fueled hydrocarbon from all the roadskimmers. Unlike the city's hush for the Test, today teemed with people.

"Let me walk you home," she said. "I want to discuss something."

Her voice was serious; her square jaw, firm. A new Queen had but one reason to talk to a new Devoted: she wanted to sound him out. She wanted him to join her Hive when they were older and more prepared. He could hardly breathe.

Jesus, he hoped that was what she wanted to talk about.

As far as he was concerned, Rhiannon was the perfect Queen. She was respectful, intelligent, and absolutely gorgeous with dark hair and a delicately pointed nose. When they argued, she mirrored his hand motions, and he knew he talked too much with his hands compared to the Dyfed-born.

She felt like home.

This could be the moment when his life revised itself for the absolute best. Rhiannon had gotten into *New Cardiff*. Maybe she would use her Test clout to suck him into the top school on the planet too. She would talk to people on his behalf—as a good Queen should—and upgrade him from generic Medical to Neurosurgeon.

She would love him and care for him, and he would worship her for the rest of their days. She would be his new church, full of truth and promise and a secure future.

"Let's go to the park instead," he said, knowing that she liked to spend time there. He didn't want her to see the dingy, dinky basement apartment he'd found when he'd moved to Dyfed at the school year's beginning. Most of his money went to his family back home. Even with two jobs, he could barely afford the space.

She wrapped his wrist with her fingers and led him across the street when the signal changed. Cold afternoon sunlight bounced off metallic atmo-scrapers and lanced Luciano's eyes. They dodged pedestrians and bicyclists, jumped away from the curb when a skimmer driver cut too close, and did so in silence until they reached the park.

The park's vibrant grass outshone his dusty, colonial memories. The oak trees dripped with flowering clusters, catkins hanging from the branches.

"My mom made me pick a tree here," Rhiannon said, her voice softer than the put-upon words suggested. "I had to dance last week on my birthday."

Luciano valiantly attempted not to envision that. Before he'd left Nuova, the parish priest had warned him about the druidic rites of the Dyfed-born. She'd have danced naked in the starlight, reaffirming her bond with the pagan gods of nature. Would he get to attend next year? Family and friends could attend those rites, he'd been told. Would it be required? What would the priest have to say about that?

Rhiannon stopped walking. Her eyes rested on his face for milliseconds before flicking everywhere else.

"I want you to join my Hive," she said. Her normally animated features were blank. Her gaze fixed firmly on his right shoulder.

She did want him! She'd seen something in him that made her pluck him from the herd. She would mark him as her own before they were separated by university and potential rivals.

She kept him from opening his mouth to accept. "Don't answer yet. It's not what you think. This isn't a Queenlet angling for your allegiance in advance. I'm asking for your Devotion *now*. I'm putting together a crew and hoping to qualify for a ship in orbit."

That was like finding that your disappointing cask of cheap white wine was actually pale ale. It wasn't what you'd expected, but it could round out a meal. After all the effort he'd made to get to Dyfed, to wend his way into the system and set up a legacy for his little sister, could he leave now? Could he give it all up?

But it wasn't *really* giving up. He'd be doing exactly what he came here for: finding the perfect Queen, one who took him seriously despite accent and upbringing, one who had respected him as a friend before they'd been cast as Queen and Devoted.

Plus, it sounded like she was trying for an Explorer ship, which came with prestige, especially if he got into xenobiology. But how would he train in the necessary arts? The Senedd certainly wouldn't offer to pay his tuition again. Would he make enough money to bring his sister to Dyfed before she got too old and corrupted by the local school systems on Nuova? Maybe Aurelia could be a Queen someday too. His thoughts whirled.

The day froze around them, springtime sun notwithstanding. Rude businessmen muttered expletives at the pair blocking the street.

Luciano broke the stillness. He thudded to his knees on the ground-stone sidewalk. "My sword and my service, my body and my blood, my agency and my anima. These all belong to you, so I swear." The traditional words of the strongest Oath, old and loyal and never to be broken.

She didn't place her hands on his shoulders or his head.

"What? You didn't!" she sputtered. "I had no idea—" She cut herself off and tried again. "Did you just swear to me in the street?"

He'd seen a scene like this in a romcom just the week before. Like its heroine, Rhiannon was still in shock.

"So I've sworn," he prompted.

She hissed through her teeth and brought her hands up to crumple the roots of her hair. *Will she reject my service? Will she reject me?* The thought sat in his stomach until he was as full as an egg.

Finally, she reached out to lace one hand's fingers through his brown-black hair. "I accept your sword and service. Your body and blood are mine to direct. Your agency and anima are my agency and anima, now and forever more. Call on me in times of trouble, as I will call on you, but always you will be my first defense."

A snake uncoiled in his stomach as she spoke the words. He didn't need to guess anymore. Formally and legally, he had his perfect Queen.

The right Queen could conquer all. She'd lead him to the glory he deserved and the money he needed for his family. Their lives would happily intertwine for all eternity, just like in the films.

She pulled him to his feet and linked their arms. He'd write that letter to his mother and sister tomorrow. He would tell them all about his new Queen.

CHAPTER FIVE

Number Six

Before another pointless post-Test class, Rhiannon checked off-campus students' Test results. They'd been posted alphabetically on a leaf-thin board in front of the school. But, of course, there wasn't enough room on the board, so the name-and-score rotated every few minutes. A-J. K-Q. R-Z.

And the Administration doesn't think that might cause traffic accidents?

To meet the minimum qualifications for the *Cauldron*, she needed one more crew member. And she didn't have any good options amongst the boys she knew.

Approaching strangers was risky, yes. They might tell someone official about her intended Hive's unorthodox makeup—*it includes a rival female, Your Honor!*—or about the sketchy Devotion levels her crew felt. Or about the fact that absolutely none of them were qualified to do anything on a spaceship.

But the alternative was going short, and that was guaranteed to fail. Oh, she supposed Victor and Gavin might know another disaffected youth. But she didn't want to rule *Victor's* Hive. She was going to have her own.

She'd been pleasantly surprised by Gavin. Did Victor understand just how well-suited to Devotion his vocally-subversive friend really was? During lunch, she'd met with him to pore over his essays. They'd talked about goals and dreams, as well as his off-planet history. For someone who didn't understand Devotion or even the local fashions, Gavin said all the right things. He trusted her judgment. He'd do well in her service, so long as the others kept him in line regarding what it meant.

After school, she and Gwyn borrowed her dad's road-skimmer and went out to visit one Alan Jones, M.Phil., M.S., number eight on the results board she'd checked that morning. Dad hadn't seemed at all worried that she wanted to check out a university in the Senedd, one that she wasn't going to attend and didn't know anybody taking classes at. If Mom were still around—

But Mom wasn't around. Hadn't been for seven years.

That was fine. Mom might even have understood why she wanted to do this thing, form this Hive. Mom might have been proud of her for agreeing to help friends in need. Mom always said loved ones came first, and she'd definitely have liked Gwyn, if they'd ever met.

Mom wouldn't have been able to help her, though,

approval or not. Four generations, and Rhiannon would be the first Queen in the family line. No Queens, no Devoted, before her.

But she came from a line of quick minds. Perceivers followed invisible threads of logic, and Rhiannon's peers had never kept up with her quick thoughts. Mom could, though. Sometimes she wondered if her mother had hidden just how good her analytical skills were, for fear that she'd be taken away from her family.

Maybe Rhiannon wasn't the first one in her family to misdirect the Test.

"This'll only take a few minutes, I hope," Rhiannon said, eyes on the road. "But after that, we'll go into the capital and check out the covered market. Won't be able to do that once we're in space, right?" Ever since they'd been old enough to go on their own, she and Gwyn made a point of getting out to the giant market once a month. Crammed with rickety booths, stacked high with silly trinkets you'd never need and precious goods you couldn't afford. The covered market always made for good looking, if not actual shopping.

Gwyn sighed. "Right," she said. Her voice was low, muffled. Unless the other girl was buried in her pad, getting an early start on no-longer-all-that-relevant homework, then something was wrong. And Rhiannon thought she might know what.

"We don't have to apply for the ship, you know. Don't let Victor talk you into things you don't want to do." *Bran's blood, it's hard to be comforting or confrontational while driving.* She hadn't liked the way Victor talked on Gwyn's behalf the day before.

"I want to." A quaver in Gwyn's voice belied the sentiment.

Rhiannon wanted to ask *Are you sure that you're sure?*, but there wasn't a good way to do that. Rhiannon knew what it meant to be a good best friend, though. She'd keep quiet and make sure Gwyn got the future she deserved.

They drove in silence. Gwyn had always been quiet, ever since they'd met in grammar school. Rhiannon had forgotten her pad at home that day, and Gwyn had tilted hers. Sharing. Like children were supposed to do. Back then, Gwyn's name was Lois, before Rhiannon had nick-named her for her white-blonde hair.

And when the teacher's wrath came down on them for socializing during a class period, Gwyn hadn't acknowl-edged the teacher's diatribe at all, soundlessly continuing to let Rhiannon read over her shoulder. Best friends ever since: Gwyn the silent support, Rhiannon the confrontationalist.

Still, Gwyn's silence held a different flavor today. A flavor that worried Rhiannon. Maybe this Hive-building wasn't a good idea.

They approached the university. When they spotted its short spires that defied the firstcomers' underground cities as well as the second wave's atmospheric domes, Gwyn exhaled loudly and rushed into a soliloquy. "It's just, I want to stay with Victor, yeah, but leave Dyfed? My family live here. And," she choked through her indecision, "what was the point of my parents' exiling my brother from our home if I'm not going to take what's been offered? I'm going to be the first person in my family since Settlement who gets to go to university, and I've got this brilliant future in animal husbandry. My parents are thrilled, more thrilled than they were the day I told them that you'd nicknamed me Gwyn." The de Vries family had celebrated their youngest's ascension to society's rarefied ranks in the most overblown way—like a proper Welsh girl. As if a name could affect Test results.

But today, neither young woman laughed at the anecdote. Because it was true. Gwyn had more options than anyone in her family for generations. Going along with Victor's scheme might make her happy in the short run but it'd ruin her family's plans. Not to mention what her brother would think.

Rhiannon chanced a look over as she drove slowly, cruising for a parking spot. Gwyn's hands were clenched on her pad, its screen dark, while she looked out the window at the roadskimmer jungle.

"Yeah, Jack got into trouble in the neighborhood, but my parents wouldn't have sent him away if they hadn't thought I was *going places.* Sometimes I wish I'd never had a brother, or met Victor, or even"—she hesitated but ploughed on—"become friends with you. If I didn't have you, the teachers wouldn't take me as seriously, and my parents would still call me Lois instead of insisting on your nickname. And I love you, and I love my life, but if I'd just been Jack Mark Two, then I wouldn't be choosing right now."

Rhiannon knew she was the only person Gwyn could or would talk to this way. It roused a warm rush of affection at the trust it implied. She *did* understand, but she couldn't make up Gwyn's mind or sort her feelings for her. She could only ensure that the other girl had choices.

Choices which Victor might deny her in his zeal for the plan.

Rhiannon parked the skimmer and turned to her best friend. "Whatever you choose to do," she vowed, "I'll make sure it's got a tidy solution. Just because I'm sounding out this Alan Jones, just because the other guys are writing essays and Devoting right and left, it doesn't mean we have to go through with this. You tell me what you want, today or tomorrow or next week, and it'll happen for you. Okay?"

Rhiannon had never felt more like a good friend, like a good family member. Never felt more like a real Queen, promising to look after someone else with all the influence she could muster. She thought of her mother, the way she'd always insisted on family loyalty.

This is my family, Mom. And she needs me.

"I can put a stop to this whole thing. No one can get a Hive ship without a Hive Queen, and the guys won't find anyone else in time." She put a hand on Gwyn's thigh, right where the paler girl's gaze rested. "The boys aren't important. They'll get over the disappointment. You just let me know what you really want."

Gwyn nodded, teary eyed, but not actually crying.

Rhiannon took that as a good sign.

"You stay here while I go meet *y dyn hwn*. Gotta keep our options open." The other girl was too delicate for strangers right now. "Take some time to think, or to write some mails, or whatever. I'll be back flash-quick."

With that, Rhiannon left the rows of skimmers behind. A campus map directed her to the university's science building. Usually on an excursion to a new place, her stomach would jump and jitter. But her successful attempt at comforting a member of her Hive reassured her. The nervous bucks weren't a bother. She could ignore them.

She didn't know for sure if this Alan Jones would be in the science building. But it seemed like the place to start hunting for a sixteen-year-old Devoted. Particularly for a potential CreaTech with two degrees, including a Master's of Science.

Inside the building, professors in faded mad-scientist coats—complete with super-tight sleeves that wouldn't dip into potions and acids—strode from room to room, mumbling deep thoughts. Students staggered behind them, loaded with overfull carryalls and odd contraptions she didn't recognize.

The floors were a much sturdier stone than the ones at her school. The ceilings appeared to be supported by knotwork columns. She had no idea how knotwork columns might function. If that wasn't an optical illusion, maybe Alan could build her something like it. If he joined her. If he specialized in spatial relations and building things.

"Excuse me." She interrupted a university student walking a little slower than the others. "Do you happen to know Alan Jones? He's about my age."

The older student growled—actually *growled*. "That bastard kicked me out of a computer lab. Three times. He's just a kid, but oooh noo. He's all the professors' favorite. Damn him."

Before she could thank him, the young man stormed off. At least she knew she was in the right place. She knew Alan liked computer labs, possibly ones in this area. She knew that people could identify him.

She traced the path her recent informant might have taken until she found something that qualified as a computer lab. Through a glass-plated door, she could glimpse rows and rows of connected stations. One whole wall was a still life of snaking wires and dancing connectors. Only two people were inside, one young and one in his seventies. They were ignoring each other. She'd take the chance that this was a free-for-all kind of place.

She walked near-silently on cushioned floors until she reached the younger looking one.

"Excuse me?"

"Augh!" He turned his seat faster than the teleportation myth. His wide shoulders were heavily muscled from lifting either weights or computer stations. Hazel eyes focused on her from a rounded face with obscenely plump lips that made her think about kissing.

Not that she wanted to kiss him. Or anyone. They'd only just met.

"Well?" he prompted.

She'd studied him for too long. She refused to blush. "Do you happen to know an Alan Jones? I'm looking for him."

Before he could answer, the older gentleman stood up.

"I'll just be leaving, then," he said. When he reached the door, he paused to give her a little bow. "Ma'am."

She wanted to ask the young man who that had been, but he didn't give her the chance. "What do you want with Alan Jones?"

Rhiannon didn't like his attitude. "None of your business." Whatever she had to say—even if she was just here to do a survey on preferred beer flavors among university students—that was for Alan's ears only. This boy had no right to pry into Alan's affairs. How did he know she wasn't his long-term girlfriend who wanted to talk about a pregnancy scare?

Whether Alan joined her Hive or not, she'd make sure he knew this kid had tried to worm into his private life.

The young man's eyes widened at her vehemence. His pink lips quirked up on the left. "It's very much my business, little girl. I'm Alan Jones."

Well, she could understand why the student in the hall hadn't liked him. It was as though he knew that calling her *little girl* would be *so* condescending, so embarrassing that she'd be tempted to leave. Just like he'd made the student in the hall leave. Had the kid really been kicked out or just annoyed out?

She wouldn't give him the satisfaction. Actually, it was funny in a cruel way. She held out a hand for him to shake.

"Rhiannon," she introduced herself, "soon to be Queen-Commander Ceridwen."

He went back to his computer screen. "No thanks. Send Professor Cantor back in if you see him."

I won't be dismissed out of hand. "No what?"

He deliberately angled the screen towards her and opened up a match-3 game. "No to whatever you want me to build for you."

"What if what I wanted to build was your own future?"

His game ended with cascading explosions. He started a new one. "Not interested in being your prodigal slave either. I've met plenty of Queen-Commanders. I'm not desperate."

He certainly had a straightforward way about him. He wasn't going to be fooled by the veneer of *Hive*, only to be disappointed when he realized just how makeshift her group was.

"I bet you have," she said. "I bet the older Queens and Commanders wanted to control you, for your own benefit, of course." She saw him stop playing, even though the timer on his game continued to count down. "I bet the younger Queens don't treat you like a real person, preferring to tease you for being a kid."

He stilled and quirked his head to the side, but he didn't look at her. He also didn't interrupt.

"I bet your funding is about to run out for your projects because soon you'll be a normal student's age instead of a curious prodigy. I bet you're interested in working on larger projects, not smaller ones, but can't get assigned or permission for anything because you're all alone and without a Queen's voice.

"I bet you *do* want to find your own Queen. One who trusts you. One who treats you like a full Hive member. One who understands that you'll be just as interested in your research as you will be in her. One who doesn't expect you to dance attendance, but who does provide structure for your days and opportunity to mingle with other brilliant people. One who will make sure those other people take you seriously as well. One who likes you for you, not for your skills or the prestige you bring her."

She stopped and waited. She didn't say *I bet you're going to join my Hive.* She'd planted the fruit tree, but would it bear citrus?

He focused on her now, with all the intensity of that brilliant mind. He'd said he'd met plenty of Queens, but had he ever met one like *her*?

"You're not a Commander at all, are you? You're a Perceiver!"

She tried to smirk mysteriously. Give the man some clues, and he'd seen through her charade. *A good sign.* "That's not what the Test says." She could fool a computerized test, but she couldn't fool a man with a lot at stake. She just had to hope that he, too, had been so frustrated by his situation that going non-traditional made sense.

The smile he gave her grew across his face, eventually making extra lines all the way back next to his jaw. "Congratulations."

She giggled, surprising herself with her delight, and perched on the table behind her. He understood! He understood what she'd done and how she'd done it. He appreciated the skill.

"Now I want to do the same for you. Join my Hive."

He shook his head. "What exactly do you want to do for me? Because I don't need you to change my Test scores."

She shrugged and leaned back on the desk to cross her legs. "I couldn't do that anyway. But I can be the Commander you need." He opened his mouth, but she cut him off. "Don't tell me you want a standard Queen instead of a Commander. Queens need so much more attention and are much less interested in helping you organize your projects and coworkers."

He nodded and gestured for her to continue.

"Here's the deal. I'm putting together a very small, very unconventional Hive. I can't promise you anything right away. We're just getting together, very young, and we're not backed by any clout other than the fact that we're a Hive. But! But I can promise to listen to whatever you tell me, to depend on you for original ideas, to make sure everyone treats you fairly, and to fight for your interests whenever you need me to."

His smile faded again. He leaned back, mocking her posture. "Will it be worth it, Perceiver-Queen?"

She tilted forward, keeping the same distance between them, as though his motion had drawn her there. He sounded disinterested. He looked disinterested. But she almost had him. She could feel it.

"I don't know," she said. "And I won't lie to you about it."

The muscles around his eyes relaxed when she refused to make false promises.

"Sold," he said. "Well, provisionally."

"Provisionally?"

"The university is required to allow each student two provisional Devotions. It's part of their public charter." His voice turned rueful. "And you're right. I really like this lab and Professor Cantor, but I'm going to be fifty before I find the Commander I need." With exaggerated grace, he fell to the floor at her feet. "I pledge you my Devotion. My life and my hands are yours for a year and a day," he swore. "May we choose never to part."

She put her hand on his brown, shaggy head. He needed a haircut, unless this was an intentional look. "I accept your life and your hands, and pledge you my consideration and attention for a year and a day. May our partnership continue forever."

Oh, I hope those were the right words for this situation. Everything she knew about this aspect of Devotion came from dubiously accurate cinema. But he rose and clasped her hands, one over the other to cement the edges of their trial period. It must've been good enough for him.

"So, what're you working on?" she asked. Now that she had him, it'd be good to find out his expertise. Maybe he even knew things about spaceships.

His reply sounded like a memorized speech. "The Myddfai-spatial tensor hypothesis is central to my dee-phil thesis. In my spare time, I work on miniaturizing

Alcubierre tensor jets and singing traditional choral pieces." His eyes widened towards this speech's end. "How can you not know this? Why didn't you know this before you came to me?"

She bit her lip to keep from grinning. "I didn't need to know what you did, only who you are."

His hands waved in the air. "What does that even mean? Sweet goddess of mercy, I've pledged myself to someone insane."

She gave up the fight to contain the grin and patted him on the shoulder. She was pretty sure he liked her a lot. "Maybe crazy is what you need."

She sidled towards the door before he could make any further arguments. "I'll let you know how things go with the ship I mentioned. We leave in a week if we get it. I'll send you the details tonight."

She made it into the hall before he shrieked again, wordless. The older gentleman, presumably Professor Cantor, was leaning against the wall. "Best of luck, Commander," he said, jerking a thumb in her new Devoted's direction.

"Thanks." That. That right there. *That* made her sure she was doing the right thing. This official, experienced person recognized something in her as a Queen and Commander. This official person believed she had the right to gather up the brilliant and irascible man inside that room. This official person hadn't kicked her out or demanded to see her credentials.

"Can you handle him like this?" she asked.

The older man just shoved his hands in his pockets and walked back into the lab, humming a tune she'd never heard. She guessed that meant *yes*.

Before rejoining Gwyn in the skimmer, she sent Gavin a quick message, letting him know the names and positions of the two crew members he'd never met. *Luciano Totti and Alan Jones, my Devoted.*

Mine. Not men already in love with someone else, like Victor. Not women or revolutionaries. These two were hers and hers alone. Devoted to their Queen-Commander.

She received Gavin's reply in moments. He'd sent the packet to the commissioning agent. She was required to report to an address in the downtown capital for in-person interview this weekend.

Back in the skimmer, she regaled Gwyn with the story of Alan's agreement, complete with an impersonation of his helpless shrieking.

She'd done it. She'd gotten them a Hive the right size to crew the *Cauldron*.

"He couldn't believe I didn't know anything about his thesis project. That's something to do with getting a degree, right?"

She and Gwyn laughed over a job well done. They ignored all the implications for the time being. They could worry later. For now, there were bizarre handicrafts and artisanal foods calling their names. The covered market beckoned.

Gwyn produced a bottle of blackcurrant from somewhere beneath her seat and took a delicate sip. Without bothering to wipe the plastic rim, she handed the bottle across to Rhiannon. Sharing drinks, sharing germs. They were self-chosen family, and family shared everything.

Just tell me what you want, Gwyn. I'll stand up to make it happen for you, just like you've always stood up for me.

CHAPTER SIX

Commander Ceridwen

Rhiannon reached the address Gavin provided at that time of morning when the sun shone at an angle that simultaneously got in your eyes and didn't actually illuminate anything.

The tiny office suite had a waiting room with thin carpets that didn't cushion the floor. A female receptionist, her lips pursed and chin tilted at a defiant angle, gestured to an area with eight orange chairs. Three other Queen or Commander hopefuls already occupied some of those chairs.

Rhiannon couldn't help but notice she was the youngest in the room by at least forty years. Oh yeah, she had a chance. Not. The interviewer would take one look at her and laugh.

She didn't know whether to feel relieved or sad. Even her most youthful rival, chewing a wad of gum and slouching like the bizarre angles of her chair didn't bother her, had to be at least eighty. Middle-aged.

The second, also eighty-ish, was more formal in a monochromatic red pantsuit. She'd braided her hair so tightly under a golden circlet-crown that her eyebrows extended to her hairline. She exuded seriousness.

The last was much older, elephant-wrinkled and paler than milk. At first Rhiannon thought she was bald, but a second inspection revealed close-cropped, thinning white hair.

Rhiannon wished she had the nerve to chop her own hair that short. Women with short hair always seemed happier and more in control of their lives. Her own shoulder-blade length, brown-black waves never seemed to get above her neck when she went to the barber. *Such a drastic change shouldn't be undertaken lightly,* her mother had cautioned when she was seven. That warning echoed in her sixteen-year-old ears, no matter how quickly any mistake might grow out.

The woman in the circlet and red pantsuit gave Rhiannon a slow evaluation, starting at her loose hair, going down to her barely heeled boots, and traveling back up again. Rhiannon did her best to ignore it. At school, the Queenlets who hoped for a Queen's Test results did the same thing all the time. Those girls tried to one-up each other with these games and psych-outs. Rhiannon stayed away from their mock-courts and proto-Hives and left them to it.

She'd never be a political, crown-and-gown kind of Queen, even after she went to university. She didn't want to separate herself too much from normal women. Sure, she'd be blessed with more options and what some called *a harem of the best men.* But she wasn't *better* than them. She couldn't go on a date or have kids without her Hive's express permission. She'd always be responsible for more than a single person ever should be. *Why did I want to be a Queen again?* She grinned to herself, but schooled her face when the red Queen glowered. *Right, because I like people and it sounded fun. Who needs to date anyway?*

Rhiannon looked over to the only non-Queen in the room. *When will the receptionist call someone into an interview?* She could definitely leave all this posturing and glowering behind.

Maybe when she was done here, she'd have a celebratory-cum-cheering-up moment and hack it all off at the barber shop. She'd leave the building with her head high, confident that she'd done her best to get the *Cauldron.* Confident that when she tried again in ten years, circumstances would align. She'd find a fashionable capital city barber to change her hair, change her image, change her into the kind of woman who didn't need *cascading locks* or *face-framing layers* to feel good about her appearance. Although, she really did like playing with the ends.

The lounging Queen snapped her gum. Rhiannon jumped, looking towards her. The gum-chewer didn't notice her attention, however. She was too busy glaring at the superior woman in red.

The crowned one sneered at the gum-snapper's antics. "They'll never give it to a slovenly thing like you. I'm going to get the ship and the prestige. You'll just be a sad, washed-up wash-out who never made it as a Queen."

Manawyddan give me strength. They're exactly like the Queenlets and Commanders-in-Training at school.

The lounging Queen stretched out further, rather than sitting up straight at the rebuke. Her slipper-shod foot nudged the bright pantsuit. The serious one brushed at imaginary dirt. "Well, I have a plan for where that ship is going, further than someone like you could ever be comfortable. What's your big plan? Mandatory hull washings?"

Can you even wash the hull of a spaceship? Would you want to risk it?

"Oh, very droll." The circlet wearer's voice dripped with contempt. She turned her ever-so-friendly attention on the eldest next. "And what about you? Will your doctors even let you go into space at your age?"

The attacked Queen inclined her head, regal and calm. The deep lines in her face gave her a gravity that the one-color-loving woman couldn't match. No energy, no negativity, nothing could withstand the gorgeous eldest's bearing. *When I'm that age, will other Queens disappear when faced with my mien?*

The most seasoned one's voice rumbled and whispered, as if her throat had rejected normal speech and could only make important noises. "I'm sure my experience and accumulated wisdom will impress the interviewers. When the ship is mine, I'll be sure to remember you and pray to the patroness, Ceridwen, for your advancement."

The words seemed gentle and serene, but Rhiannon couldn't help snorting. The glorious one *could* have meant *praying for your advancement into obscurity* or some other destination that would keep the red pantsuit far, far away from the *Cauldron*'s path through the stars.

The three Queens swiveled their heads, hare-quick, to home in on new prey. They'd happily ignored her until she'd made a noise. Now it was too late for renewed silence. They had the scent of fresh insecurity and would peck away at her until they laid her meager confidence bare for the massacre.

"What a sweet little girl," gushed the one in red. "Where's your mother?"

Dead, actually. Well, if this Queen planned to come after her for her age, she'd show her appreciation in the way only a younger person could. She raised her eyebrows and furrowed them down the middle, then pulled her head back onto her neck as though repulsed or doing a proper sit-up. From the way the older woman cringed back, Rhiannon knew she'd succeeded in making the derisive *Did you seriously just say that to me?* face that she'd seen on her more critical peers. *A teenager can out bitch-face you any time, Queenie. Don't try that tactic with me.*

The eldest cocked her head, more curious than cruel. Perhaps she found it as difficult to gauge Rhiannon's age as the other way around. As far as Rhiannon knew, this woman had been one of Dyfed's first Queens, self-made and just as untrained as herself. "Why do you think you deserve *Ceridwen's Cauldron*?" She caressed the name like a familiar friend, barely pronouncing the *r* in the second word.

Were they really going to make her join their posturing? "My Hive members are young, yes, but eager," she said. "We want to see the universe, starting near home and working our way out. Our strong desire for exploration bonds us together." *Weakly, perhaps.*

The eldest Queen rolled her head onto her chest, so Rhiannon couldn't see her reaction. Her neck cracked like breaking bones.

The lounging Queen looked away. Her skull upturned to the ceiling, she ran restless hands over the smooth plastic beneath her.

The red pantsuit wearer didn't talk, didn't move, didn't show any signs of life as she focused on her judgment of Rhiannon's worth. Then she took a noisy breath, spared the room a last sneer, and primly folded herself into the orange monstrosity farthest from Rhiannon's corner.

The pantsuit's rustling shook the eldest Queen from her stupor. She levered herself from her chair.

"You two." She pointed at the middle-aged women. "You're dismissed." Not checking to see that her orders had been followed, she stalked off through the only doorway, leaving the remaining three hopefuls in silence.

Rhiannon and the other Queens looked to each other. Should the older two really leave? Did that mean that

Rhiannon should too? The lounging one shrugged and tilted back to better ignore her rivals.

The receptionist's officious voice cut through the confused silence. "Rhiannon?"

Rhiannon raised her hand.

"Through there." The receptionist pointed through the doorway the majestic Queen had already taken.

Oh, thank goodness. Interview time arrived. She could go in, be judged as too inexperienced, told thank-you, and allowed to go home. With or without the haircut. The important part was to vacate this terrible coffin-room. To get out of here.

Walking across the lobby, she felt wet, cool pools at her armpits. She clamped her arms closer to her body to hide the evidence of her nerves.

She stopped in the doorway to look back at the others. The receptionist was bending over a pad and pointing out something to the other two applicants, who didn't appear to notice that they were being herded towards the exit. Had they actually been dismissed?

Rhiannon strode through the doorway now, more ready than ever to get this over with. Who cared how hot her core temperature got? Proving her unfitness for space exploration wouldn't matter. Her Hive wasn't going to get the ship anyway.

The oldest Queen was sitting behind a sheet metal desk, bare exccpt for a few pads overlapping each other in a messy pile. The dark, deep lines around her mouth turned into caverns when she smiled. Her perfect, pearly teeth were flat and herbivore smooth. She consulted a pad perched atop the rickety pile. "Rhiannon, eh? A good strong name for a Queen."

What's in a name? She stifled a giggle at the thought. *Not the time, Rhiannon.*

The beautiful, scary woman picked up the pad and pressed her thumb to a page. She hit a few buttons, pressed her thumb again, and tossed the pad Rhiannon's way. *Should I pick it up?* "Congratulations, Captain Ceridwen. I've made my decision. You are now the Queen-tenant of *Ceridwen's Cauldron*."

Rhiannon plucked the rubber-frictioned pad from the desk. It trembled in her hands, but didn't fall. She stared at the words, at the box waiting for her thumbprint.

"You didn't even read my essays, or check that I had enough people."

The Queen laughed like a river in a book about Earth topography, constantly refreshing and stronger than it looked. "I didn't have to. Weren't you in that waiting room with me? You were the only Queen who said *we*. You considered your Hive first, not yourself. That's the mark of a true Queen."

Rhiannon shook her head, still looking at the empty printbox. She'd seal her future with print and DNA. Sweaty rivulets curled the hair under her ears. "It's Commander, actually." Perhaps being the administrative, some said *overbearing,* Commander type would disqualify her. Perhaps only the gentle, attention-seeking Queens were allowed to tenant the *Cauldron*.

"You'll be fine," the woman said.

Bumpy, moist warmth grabbed Rhiannon's hand. The older Queen lifted her thumb for her and pressed it to the box.

"Done!" She smiled her deep, cavern smile again. "Congratulations, *Commander* Ceridwen. May your run be as good as mine."

This was the former Captain Ceridwen? Maybe that meant she'd seen something in Rhiannon, seen something that made her seem a qualified Commander. Seen something that meant Rhiannon wasn't a fraud. Seen something that proved she had the right characteristics. "And you get to decide this? Not some administrator or government official?"

The venerable lady river-laughed again. "The old captain always gets to pick the new one. It's tradition. So long as the ship's spaceworthy and not slated for a particular purpose. These old darlings aren't good for much more than training a Hive crew, you know." She leaned across the desk again, conspiratorial. Rhiannon clenched her hands defensively. "The Senedd hopes your experience will inspire you with the vastness of possibility. When you outgrow the *Cauldron,* you might choose to join a battlefleet or become exobiologists."

"When?" Rhiannon was pretty sure she was asking when the former Captain Ceridwen had become Captain and what things were like back in those first days, but she couldn't find the right words.

"I'll have my crew out tomorrow, so you can take possession immediately. We've been packing all week." The former Captain Ceridwen must have seen the dismay on her face. She rushed to reassure her replacement. "I'll arrange your first run, and the government will help you organize any others. But a young thing like you probably doesn't want to do all mail and diplomatic couriers, eh?" She patted Rhiannon on the shoulder and guided her to the exit with a strong hand. "You'll be fine or my name isn't Olivia Jones."

But the woman's name wasn't Olivia Jones. It was Captain Ceridwen! Or, it had been until a moment ago. Until Rhiannon had signed the paperwork. Now the old woman was Olivia Jones again.

And now Rhiannon was Commander Ceridwen. With a Hive to inform. So much for homework and haircuts.

CHAPTER SEVEN

Hand It Over

The group walked on a carpeted trail from the space-port's main concourse out to the *Cauldron*. Victor held Gwyn's hand in his, tangling their fingers together. They'd never dared do that in public before. But here in Dyfed's orbiting spaceport, no one knew them. No one knew Victor was Devoted. Or that Gwyn wasn't his Queen. Here, they could be a happy couple like any other.

Ahead of them, Rhiannon tucked a hand into Gavin's voluminous sleeves, ostensibly resting it on an elbow.

Victor tilted his head down an inch to Gwyn's ear. "They're getting along well, don't you think?"

Gwyn hummed vaguely. Victor stopped contemplating his new Queen to see what had grabbed his girl-friend's attention. The walls around them alternately proclaimed safety messages—*Fire Exit Keep Clear / Allanfa*

Dan Cadwch Yn Glir—with chances to be involved in the station's upcoming Beltane Revelry. *Sign Up Here to Jump the Flames / Gofrestru i Neidio y Fflamau.*

"Do you want to go?" he asked her, pointing to one of the latter signs.

She shrugged and swung their hands like a pleased child. "They probably won't have real fires," she said. "Not on the orbital."

He gestured to another poster of a red-hot bonfire in an oak grove. *Cleanse yourself for Beltane.* "They clearly have something." He raised her bony knuckles to his lips and pressed a whispery kiss to them. "Let's do it. To start this new adventure right."

She'd stolen the air from his lungs and hidden it between her teeth. "Okay." The smile she gave him filled his whole world.

He stared, transfixed by her sparkling teeth, breathless before her hair, paler than snow. She was a creature of legend. Blodeuwedd come to make his life complete, and nevermind how badly *that* story turned out for all concerned. How could he ever have imagined a life without Gwyn? What horrible fate would have seized his fragile heart in its claws if Rhiannon hadn't been ready to help?

Their steps' rhythm lulled Victor into a comfortable mental stillness. Gwyn always calmed him. She gave him darkness and the space for thought. He nearly tripped over his own feet when she came to a stop. "What?" he asked.

Once again, Victor followed her gaze. *Ah, we've arrived.* Outside the airlock for the docking spoke to the

Cauldron, an old woman waited. Victor could see her shockingly white hair past Gavin and Rhiannon's shoulders. It wasn't white with pale beauty like Gwyn's, but with age. She wore her years like a majestic cloak, but he didn't want to talk with her if he could avoid it. She might guess too much.

The woman spoke. Her voice creaked like a chair about to fall apart. "Commander Ceridwen."

Rhiannon raised her chin in regal acknowledgement, but her voice sounded comparatively high and unsure. "Queen Olivia."

Fuck! A Queen! Victor dropped Gwyn's hand and hoped the official woman hadn't noticed his lapse. He slid in front of his girlfriend, hoping he might be tall enough to shield her from the stranger's view. Gwyn's cool hand touched his back, pouring calm into his soul.

He bared his teeth in a smile and prayed to his patron god that it could pass for normal. *I'll leave an offering in your name, Lleu Llaw Gyffes. Just please. Please let us pull this off. Don't let this person notice Gwyn and call her out as a disruptive influence to a new Hive.*

His prayers appeared answered. The croaking Queen didn't so much as look at Rhiannon's entourage. She said, "We've cleared the ship out, down to the plates and the Kevlar. We left you some oxygen-bearing plants and the mattresses. What would we do with those? It's a clean slate." Her eyes twitched to indicate the millions of boxes on a palette at her side. Victor twitched with her, unsure where to move to stay between Gwyn and discovery.

66

A blossoming heat radiated from his sternum and pulled his awareness away from the danger. Back to his own body. Matching Gwyn's still, cool hand on his back, Rhiannon's rested like a fiery blanket across his chest. His Queen had this under control. He could simply focus on the prodigious load of boxes and wonder how the old crew had fit all their stuff on that ship.

Their ship now.

Victor leaned into the pressure on his solar plexus, breathing deeply to feel the push against his Queen's skin. She was the warmth of spring. He exhaled, expanding his chest into her palm and reveling in the cozy Hive dynamic. But that also pushed his hind ribs against his girlfriend's icy hand.

He flashed cold, and bumps rose on his skin under his tunic. He caught himself before he shrunk away from both women, but only just. If the old Queen noticed his sudden change in behavior, she might also notice the girl he obscured. *Gwyn! Do I betray you when I let another woman touch me?* But Rhiannon wasn't another *woman*. No, she was a *Queen*. Victor's Queen at that.

He was supposed to touch her, supposed to take comfort in her presence. If he didn't let affection for her eclipse all else, how was he supposed to build a new family in this strange Hive? Then again, they were a *very* strange Hive.

Gods. She wasn't even really his Queen. He hadn't Devoted yet.

His eyes slid to the boxes behind the stranger. They

towered over her in squares and cylinders. Would he amass that much *stuff* someday?

Rhiannon's hand left his chest when she walked closer to the old woman. Victor's lungs expanded on the side where her touch had been. They were still tight where Gwyn rested behind him. *I'm destined to be a terrible Devoted, a terrible boyfriend. Just like my father.*

Rhiannon and the other Queen stood apart from Victor and Gwyn and Gavin, embroiled in some pleasantries he couldn't hear. Those culminated in small bows to each other, neither deeper than her mirror's.

Wishing them "*Pob lwc*," the crone went on her way. *Good luck.* Victor was going to need it.

The path cleared. Gwyn bounded ahead, no doubt remembering the Queen's comment about leaving oxygen-bearing plants. Gwyn loved plants. And Victor loved Gwyn. At least, he thought he did. He'd done everything for her, for their love. But, in that case, how could he respond to Rhiannon's touch?

His pad vibrated. A message from Gwyn. Already? She'd just left him seconds ago. *So much green down here! And MOLD.* He laughed, and if the sound was shaky, that was no one else's business.

Soon Gavin was laughing with him, for his own reasons. Their peals rang through the hub's spoke. The sound of freedom and love and a whole life ahead of them. Gavin wrapped his arm around Victor's shoulders. The pair of them staggered after Gwyn into their new home.

CHAPTER EIGHT

It's In the Manual

Luciano had passed through Dyfed's orbiting space-port before, when he'd first arrived from Nuova. Then he'd been impressed by its dust-free cleanliness and brightly-lit schedule boards. Now he paid its corridors scant attention, eager to board his new ship-home for the first time.

Unchallenged by any security officials, he entered the *Cauldron* via her docking spoke. Her small, bare corridors gave no clues to the ship's size or layout. He was grateful the old crew had painted blue arrows on grey bulkheads to help the newcomers explore.

His boots banged a steady rhythm against the steel-and-Kevlar floors. Those floors matched equally uncov-ered walls—blank except for metal panels that kept the ship's innards from spilling onto unforgiving ground.

After he met with Rhiannon, he'd see if Medical was just as gutted and unfinished. Hopefully all the necessities would be stocked.

She'd set the location for their one-on-one as the pilot house, so he climbed the metal rungs to it. A room only meant for one person, maybe two if they squeezed, already warm. After the bare corridors with their frigid hostility, Rhiannon's presence and body heat lent a coziness to the space. Every available surface was coated and crammed with instrumentation. No one had skimped on *equipment* in this room, for all that the pilot's chair had no cushioning.

His perfect Queen leaned over the console in front of the pilot's chair and looked up to greet him with sparkling eyes. Her face was flushed, and her hand came up to push an errant hair behind her ear. Her usually meticulous eyeliner was smudged from the heat and the work.

"Hi, Luciano," she said.

Pinkened, disheveled, streaked. She'd never looked more beautiful.

"Hi." He looked forward to years upon years of her energy and vision, God willing.

He climbed the last rung and found himself nearly pressed against her. He could smell the maple that lingered in her clothes and the inoffensive chemical she used in her hair.

"I'm glad you made it." Her bright smile lanced through his chest like the Spear of Longinus.

He'd do anything to keep her happy. He'd bring her his best accomplishments. He'd discover a new species with attendant antibiotics. He'd make her happy forever, his Queen.

"I'll always come when you call," he said. It was part of his oath, after all. "I can't tell you what we need in Medical yet, sorry. I've only just arrived. But I'll get on that as soon as we've finished here."

He'd show her how good he was at his job, even though they'd had to leave school at sixteen. He knew his stuff so far. Plus he'd learn more from books and exploration and local practitioners they met along the way.

"Ah, about that." She looked away from him. Her right hand twisted in her silky, near-black strands, while the other rooted around beneath the main console and pulled out a very thick, very physical book. It was so heavy that her fingers shook and the tendons in her hand stood out, outlining musculature and veins.

He plucked the book from her grip with his stronger hands. Although the cover looked old, the pages had never been opened. Outdated fonts proclaimed it *Manual Pilot Manual: Best of the Century!!!* The tome rested in his hands like a new *Bible*, a single block full of important information that had yet to be cracked and explored. *Strange that it's not on a pad. Maybe if a pilot needs to use it, that means the power's gone out?*

He wished she'd look directly at him again, the way she had when he'd come in. Maybe he could tease her into paying attention to him. God, he was never as real on his own as he was when she included him in her world.

"Taking up manual stimulation?" he asked slyly.

God in Heaven, Luciano! He couldn't believe he'd said that out loud. The joke, weak enough on its own double-entendre'd feet, wasn't something one should say to a lady, much less to a Queen. He closed his eyes against whatever condemnation she might muster. He stood blind for a moment, breathing in muggy disapproval and twitching towards her for comfort. He pulled himself away when their skin touched.

Her hands closed around his on the book's covers, imparting forgiveness and a bit of sweat. She squeezed. His shoulders relaxed even as his fingers contracted around the *Manual Pilot Manual.*

"I need you to do me a favor." Her voice was lower-pitched now, not the happy chirp of greeting from moments before. Nor was it the deadly deep anger he'd once heard her unleash on a vicious schoolgirl Queenlet who wouldn't let a freshman buy a drink from the vending machines until he'd abased himself before her.

Luciano opened his eyes to sink into her obsidian pupils. Was this how the prophets felt when confronted with Jesus, when they realized who he was and submersed themselves in His wisdom and love? "Anything," he agreed, not needing to hear what the favor might be. "You know that." He tried to put his conviction and devotion into his voice and his gaze.

She tapped the book in his hands. Her fingernail clicked against the shiny, thick cover. "I need you to read up on this and become our pilot."

If he played pilot for a bit, for his Queen's sake, who would be taking over in Medical? What if someone got hurt?

"I need you, Luciano." She leaned forward earnestly, tilting her head more aggressively when the space between them became too small for her to keep his gaze otherwise. "Gods know this isn't fair to you, but you're the only one I can trust. We've been project partners often enough that I know you can get through the theoretical and into the practical better than anyone else on board."

Except for herself, of course. He'd seen her fly through physics books and come up with the lab ideas that had been invented by geniuses a hundred years after the last thing she'd read about. He knew she could do the same for history, literature, and—doubtless—piloting too.

She continued, "It's only temporary. Someone needs to be first, after all, and we leave the spaceport right after Beltane to ferry our first passenger. Once you get things running and then teach me, we can spell each other on piloting while you take over Medical as you were meant to. I'll teach the next replacement myself."

He spared a moment's jealousy for the next student who would get to spend hours crammed into the pilot house with his sweet, glowing Queen. But Luciano would get to do it first and be seen as her ship-wide expert. Still...

"Of course I'll help you." He rested his own hand over hers, now atop the book, promising his strength in body as well as in mind. "But if someone needs me in Medical, what will we do?"

She pulled her hand away and tugged on her tunic's sapphire hem. It scraped his trousers where their legs stood near enough for the fabrics to touch. "Well, you haven't had the chance to meet our sixth crew member yet. But number six is really good with animals and even spent time volunteering with vets last summer."

Humans and animals had much in common. That might work out for a little while. "Will he want to give up Medical later, then? I can share, you know."

She bit her lip and looked away. Was she going to ask him to stay away from Medical permanently?

"No, no. It'll be fine. Number six will just handle things until you take over. Number six prefers plants and animals and will focus on the gardens and carbon scrubbers once we're all settled. I'll introduce you at dinner."

The book in Luciano's hands made his forearms ache. He let one arm take its full weight, holding it against his leg. He couldn't remember the last time he'd seen a physical textbook. It hadn't been on Dyfed, surely, though they still had them on the mining planet where he'd grown up.

"I look forward to it," he said. He thudded into the pilot's chair and opened the book to the table of contents. "I'll be fine." He shooed her from the pilot house. God knew she probably had things to do. Plus, he needed to get used to being alone in this cramped box. She clambered down the metal rungs, leaving him to his book and his charge.

He'd make his Queen proud. He'd do his duty as King of the Pilot House.

***

Eventually, though, Luciano needed to eat. Deep down, he could also admit that he needed a break. He could only read for so long, whether or not he was holding a physical book, before his brain needed some outside stimulation. Besides, Rhiannon hadn't ordered him to remain in the pilot house while reading the manual. She'd only tasked him with understanding it.

He tossed the book down to the main floor as gently as he could and descended the ladder after it. So long as he took it with him, he was still working. He was just working in a different place. Somewhere around here there had to be a kitchen. He could read when he found it.

The endless cold corridors, painted with arrows, seemed to stretch for miles. He'd seen a schematic. He knew the corridors in the crew areas were barely a kilometer, all told. Maybe being lost made a difference in perceived distance?

He dreamed that when he reached the cafeteria, Rhiannon would be waiting for him. She'd be in the center of a red-and-gold painted room, majestic. As he approached, she'd sense him first as a tremble in her personal space. She'd open her arms wide to welcome him, like a painting of Mary. No, like a lover greeting her dearest one after long absence.

He shook his head to get that thought out. It wasn't allowed. Queens didn't take lovers from among their Hives. Some never took a lover at all, choosing instead to donate ova to keep up the population stock. They couldn't show favoritism. It corrupted a Hive's dynamic. What he desired could, alas, never be.

But like all Devoted who started their tenures with a romantic love instead of a platonic one, he'd grow out of it. Days and years would pass. They would become family. Maybe, twenty years from now, the Hive as a whole would feel that it was time for Rhiannon to have a child. Maybe, in that hypothetical future, they'd decide Luciano should be the father. Or, perhaps the others would grow out of any romantic attachment, and suggest that Luciano—ever constant—should take on that lover's role.

It wasn't something to worry about now. Now he only had to worry about making a sandwich.

Luckily, he'd finally found the right room. At least, it looked like he had. It was bigger than the others he'd peeked into, though it had the same bare floors and empty walls as the rest of the ship. A young man sat on an unpadded bench at the bare steel table in the room's center.

The young man didn't look up when Luciano entered. He stayed hunched over his pad, tapping at its screen. Beside him, a half-eaten sandwich sat on a disposable plate, probably taken from one of the restaurants in the spacedock's main concourse. "That doesn't make any sense!"

The man slapped a hand down on the metal table, then shook out his fingers.

Luciano couldn't help but notice that those fingers were almost as dark as his own. On a ship full of extra-pale Dyfed natives, Luciano hadn't expected to see anyone as dark as he. He wondered what the others looked like. *There are six of us, and I only know Rhiannon for sure. And now this man.*

"Hello," he said. No need to lead the dog into the yard. They both had a place on this ship.

The man jumped. His mouth's surprised O made his round face almost comic. "What do you want?"

Luciano crossed to sit beside him. "I just came for a break. Maybe I can help you with whatever you're working on?"

"I doubt it." He didn't sound annoyed, merely dismissive, as though he didn't trust Luciano's ability to understand. He tilted the screen to show a graph. The first half described an exponential curve, and the second half abruptly fell off. "What do you know about power curves for Alcubierre tensor jets? As you can see from the graph, everything starts out fine. And then we die as soon as we achieve twice light speed." His voice's deep thrum took up residence in Luciano's bones.

Luciano had been reaching for the pad, but pulled his arms back. "I haven't got a clue," he admitted. His fingers twisted with one another. "I'm good at math, though." They were supposed to be Hive mates. They rallied to Rhiannon's banner, but without their own bonds, the whole Hive would fall apart and tear their Queen to pieces in the process. Couldn't they at least try to bond?

The man rolled his eyes. "Good at math?" The way he said it implied that *everyone* was good at math and he didn't really need Luciano's help. Still, they were *Hive mates*. "Couldn't hurt to test you out. This one is for Hawking field stability."

Luciano shrugged. The theory was beyond him, but if the data came from a simulation... "Can I see the equations?"

The man handed over his pad. Everything looked a jumble. He recognized a Hamiltonian in there, but the rest was beyond him. He didn't have the background. This was why he needed to go to university. He'd get there someday.

"Sorry." He passed the pad back. "I guess I can't help you after all."

The man shrugged. "*Diolch*," he said. "You tried."

Luciano knew that word. *Thanks*. This man was better than just Dyfed-born, then. He was true Welsh. The original families' descendants tended to use the language unthinkingly. Luciano had managed to join a Hive with a Welsh Queen and at least one Welsh member! Only in his wildest dreams, the ones where his Test results had made him a neurosurgeon—not just a general medical practitioner—could he have joined a real Welsh Hive.

"Ugh." The man tossed his pad onto the bench beside him. It clattered on the bare metal. "We could use some cushions, I think."

As a conversational gambit, it was better than nothing. "I'm going to the Quartermaster's office tomorrow. I could pick some up." *I'd invite him to come with me, but what's his name?* "I'm Luciano." He held out his hand to shake.

The man tilted his head to the right and regarded him. *This is weird.* "It suits you." He nodded. "I'm Alan." He took Luciano's hand and tugged him into an awkward half-hug. *I'm not the only one trying to bond with a Hive mate. That's something.* "The equations are for a tensor jet I'm building."

Where was he building it? Those didn't fit on ships this size. Did they?

"Aren't those the size of the Senedd building?"

Alan's lips curled smugly upward on the left. He gave up on holding in his happiness, and broke into a pleased laugh. Somehow, it made his wide nose look even bigger. "Yep. If I can manage this, everyone will acknowledge my genius. I'll get a Science and Technology Eisteddfod Medal to present to our Queen."

"I'll leave you to it." Luciano had his own work to do.

He was halfway to the door when Alan called out, "Hey, d'you want the rest of this sandwich? Don't want to waste it."

Luciano turned to give the other Devoted an incredulous look. It didn't do much good. Alan was back to hunching over his pad, not tracking the outside world. *I did come here to eat something.* But for all that Hives were families, they just weren't there at the point of eating each other's discarded food yet.

"I'm not hungry. I just wanted to stretch my legs." He could read the *Manual Pilot Manual* somewhere else. The pilot house was empty and quiet at the moment. This had been a good start.

CHAPTER NINE

Transitivity of Friendship

Rhiannon knew friendship didn't have transitive properties. Knew she couldn't expect her childhood friends to immediately adore her new ones. But she hadn't expected the Hive's first dinner together to be so awkward.

The air carried essence of roast lamb, delivered to the ship by a spaceport restaurant. The scent was familiar, but cut through with a sharp acidity. Luciano's tomato-based, Italian-style meal fought for airspace with the savory Dyfed-style the rest had ordered.

Sure, she'd expected Gwyn, Victor, and Gavin to all sit together, even if she'd wished Gwyn might sit with *her*. Sure, she'd expected everyone to have different tastes and interests. But she'd also expected them to make an effort.

So far, that hadn't happened.

She inhaled deeply, demonstrating her waning patience to anyone who cared to notice. And *that* ought to have been everyone. What with her being their Queen and Commander and all.

Bunched together at the metal table's end, the three already-friends shared bread for dunking in their mint sauce. The cavernous room could fit more than a mere six crewmen, but those three seemed determined to squeeze into a tiny space. To ignore everything outside their corner.

Their steadfast avoidance didn't keep her other two Devoted from noticing them. Alan shifted as close to Rhiannon as possible, sensing that the bubble of solidarity excluded him. She hoped that this wasn't going to be *Rhiannon's Hive versus Victor's Friends.* She should never have let him bring Gavin. Yes, Gavin had been the impetus, but his presence skewed the balance.

Luciano had yet to taste his steaming tomato-whatever. His eyes were riveted on Gwyn. When Rhiannon had made introductions, Luciano had whispered, "Number Six?" He hadn't said anything since. His mouth formed a small trapezoid, pulling his face out of alignment and making it into an unhappy caricature.

Rhiannon took a bite of her lamb, sucking out its juices. Was getting along too much to ask? She didn't demand that they eat the same food or have the same interests. She simply wanted them to speak with one another. With Alan overwhelmed and Luciano on mute, the overture would have to come from the Hive-within-a-Hive.

Catching Gavin's eye, she gave him her best glare, lowering her inner brows and narrowing the corners of her eyes until she felt mean. He jumped in his seat. He put a protective hand over his Tribute packet on the table. He looked behind him to see if she could be glaring at someone else. *No, really. There's no one there, Gav.*

His shoulders hunched so far forward that his tunic and vest rumpled. He put down the bread on its way to his mouth and played with the frayed ends of his belt. "So, ah, I did this efficiency thing with the oxygen tanks today. It ought to improve their airflow."

Finally! Someone was talking! She flashed Gavin a wide, grateful smile. He preened under her regard, shoulders straightening. His permanent semi-smile filled out into the real thing. He brought a hand up to duck behind it in blushing pleasure.

Alan gulped loudly, taking down a too-large mouthful without chewing it. "I'd like to see the designs for that, if you don't mind."

The conversation might have gone all right if it hadn't been for the *if you don't mind* tacked on the end. Gavin's expression went from pleased accomplishment to defensive in a half-second.

"You don't trust my work?" His voice was slow and dangerous. "You think you could do better?"

The conversation might have gone all right if it hadn't been for the *you think you could do better?* Alan could have apologized at that point. He could've made noises about how the words came out wrong and how all he wanted was to bond with a Hive mate, maybe learn something. But Rhiannon knew as soon as she heard *you think you can do better?* that the situation was beyond salvaging.

Alan wasn't going to lie.

"Yes." Alan sounded casually surprised, as though he wondered why the question was necessary. Whether or not he meant to start a fight, he wasn't going to back away from one. Alan didn't hide. He didn't do social niceties. It was why she knew he'd Devote to her in the first place. He'd refused to hide behind a Queen who would try to control him.

And he was better at theoretical-to-practical engineering than anyone she'd ever met in university. "I mean, I'm sure you did a good job." He seemed to have realized that he shouldn't sound quite so arrogant, but it sounded very *damning with faint praise.*

"Know a lot about airflow, do you?" Gavin pressed him, taking advantage of the backtracking. A bumpy line formed in the left side of his forehead, indenting straight from brow to hairline. "You're an expert in the field?"

Alan spread his palms up on the table and leaned away. "Well, no, but—"

Gavin didn't give him a chance to talk about his experience in fluid dynamics. "So let's just assume that I might have done things right," he growled. The words hung in the air before he shrugged, content to forget all about the argument now that he'd won. With a self-deprecating smile he told Victor and Gwyn, "It's like a water feature effect I helped put together while my mom was doing *The*

Tempest over in English space."

His sudden easygoing attitude didn't fool Rhiannon. If she couldn't fix this somehow, Alan and Gavin would end up hating each other with the passion of a thousand epic poets.

Gwyn put her elbows on the table and asked in her musical, high-pitched voice, "We're not going into English space, are we?"

By the gods, Rhiannon loved her best friend for getting them all onto a new conversational track. Good thing it was about their future, too, because Rhiannon really needed to figure this out: where *were* they going? And what was she going to do when they got there?

Victor laughed in response to Gwyn's question, as though the idea were ridiculous and of course they wouldn't. He stopped when he realized he was the only one. Slouching and blotchy-faced, he tried to sound reasonable. "I guess we might have to pass through."

Gavin bumped Victor's shoulder, cajoling the latter out of his embarrassment. Rhiannon wished she knew how to do that with just a touch. "On our way to where, d'you think? I filled out our application essays with plans to do free trading in multiple systems, working our way to see the universe." He favored them all with a half-leer, half-condescending grin. "Goodness knows you Dyfed-born could use a Grand Tour."

Victor was well on his way to frown-y slouching again at that. Apparently, Gavin's extraplanetary love didn't enthuse his friends. Gwyn looked uncomfortable too, but

Rhiannon couldn't tell how Luciano felt yet. He still stared mutely at Gwyn. His food was getting cold.

Considering the recent altercation, support for Gavin's proposal came from an unexpected quarter.

"Yes!" Alan stood up in his excitement, bumping his hip against the table with a dull reverberation. "Extrasystem trading will raise money that we can use to buy our own labs and any favors we want on Dyfed." His hands came up beside his ears and slashed the air to punctuate his words. Somehow, Rhiannon could tell this was the positive kind of arm waving, not the frustrated kind. "We could see the universe, then settle back home."

Huddling away from the loud passion, Victor and Gwyn clasped hands. Their food forgotten, they tried to slide into each other. They weren't hiding their love affair, but Alan was charmingly oblivious to the repercussions, too excited by his own plans.

Gavin wasn't watching his friends either. He was reluctantly accepting the help from Alan. "Not sure I'd want to settle on Dyfed, but I'll have decades of exploration to convince you there are better places."

The words were friendly, but the tone and gritted teeth gave them a bite. A bite that said Gavin knew more. A bite that threatened to restart their earlier fight, even if they were currently in agreement on this issue. Still, she appreciated the insinuation that Gavin and Alan would both be around for decades to come.

Victor pulled Gwyn into his lap. Her tunic rustled as he caressed her shoulders and upper arms. He looked totally relaxed, but Rhiannon could see the muscles like sticks in his skinny neck. "I'm with Gavin. Dyfed might not be the best final destination. We were thinking of a farming planet, or just staying on the ship forever." His body made it clear that *we* included Gwyn, who didn't contradict him.

"Farming?" Alan's incredulous voice sliced through the brewing consensus. "No, no, no." He paced and wheeled his arms through the air at breeze-making speeds. "You!" He snapped fingers at Gavin. "Airflow boy! Back me up on this."

The request might have gone all right if it hadn't been for the *Airflow boy*.

Gavin stood and halted Alan's frenzied circle of the room. He body-checked the physicist prodigy and towered over him, all ropy muscles and barely veiled danger.

"Gavin," he ground out.

Alan stumbled back. "What?"

Gavin slid forward, insinuating himself between Alan and any help that might've come from the table. "My name is Gavin."

Some Queen I am. The first time my Hive gets together, it's going to end in bloodshed. Clever Manawyddan, how am I supposed to talk them down? Then again, Manawyddan wouldn't know. Even if he was real. Even if he could talk. That was one god who got beat up a lot, while still being the smartest and the best.

Thankfully the situation didn't devolve.

It didn't get the chance.

Luciano moved for the first time since meeting Gwyn. He slammed his fist into his tomato-whatever forcefully enough to shudder the steel table. With a dripping, red finger, he pointed at Gwyn. "You snake!" His voice was a red dragon, pounding their ears with its ferocity.

Was he upset that Gwyn was a woman or that she'd taken over Medical from him?

Slow, deliberate, he flicked the tomato and cheese from his finger. It landed far short of its destination, but Gwyn still recoiled. Victor turned, too late, to shield her body with his own.

Luciano smeared the remains on a serviette, even as he leveled an accusing look on Rhiannon. "Just what did you intend for this ship anyway?"

Rhiannon could only shrug. She didn't really have any intentions for the ship.

His mouth gaped wide, trapezoidal and angry and helpless. He pulled himself together to give her a flat non-smile. He snatched his manual from its place on the table, turned on his boot heel, and walked out.

Stunned silence fell. Victor and Gwyn made their excuses, off to spend time alone. Together. Rhiannon wished she had someone to spend some time alone with. It used to be Gwyn for her too. Before Victor came around.

Gavin and Alan shuffled back to the table, keeping a few feet between them and not looking at each other.

Gavin said, "I'm going to clear a space to practice some stage combat. You're welcome any time." They all know he only meant one of them.

Then, it was just Alan and Rhiannon, alone in the sudden quiet. The dining room was a ghostly shadow. They sat on their empty benches amidst the detritus of a meal no one had finished eating.

Alan retook his seat beside her. "So. My lady." He dug a bread chunk into his congealing lamb stew. "What do you really want to do with the ship?"

She supposed she should have expected him to ask. After all, she was Queen. She was *Commander*. The impetus and the decision should have been hers. But she hadn't really wanted the ship. Nor a Hive just yet. She'd wanted to go to New Cardiff and become a Queen on her own time. She'd wanted to help a friend. Anything for a friend. Good thing she only had the one.

Rhiannon stood. "I'm going to do some research about owning a ship. Don't tell the others, but I haven't really thought this through."

Alan laughed briefly and reached for her hand. "This must be the first time in your life you haven't evaluated all the angles and data." Dry, raspy breadcrumbs stuck to his skin with sticky, savory stew. But she couldn't be upset at the mess he transferred to her. He'd *reached* for her, instead of eating or ignoring. "If, if you're feeling lost, you can come to me and talk about whatever you need to." He squeezed.

"Unless I'm really busy," he added.

She chuffed her amusement, worried that if she chose a longer sound, it might turn into a sob instead of a laugh.

"Don't worry about me," she said. "I promised to be a

Commander, and not a needy Queen, didn't I?" She shook her head and made her way to the door. "Have fun working on something personal tonight. Learning more about the ship can wait until tomorrow."

His mouth was full when he answered. "Sure. Just don't expect me to finish off my miniaturized tensor jet anytime in the next decade."

You never have to finish a personal project, just enjoy it. Rhiannon nodded to him and left the dining room. She was *leaving*. It wasn't a *retreat*. Not even when all she planned to do was get to her cabin, curl up on her bed, and read everything she could find about where the ship could go next.

Maybe she couldn't solve her Hive's interpersonal problems, but she could figure out what they'd do once the infighting stopped.

Chapter Ten

Rituals

Luciano started his morning with a jog around the *Cauldron*. He could get in a good five kilometers if he did eight circuits of the residential areas. After getting a full night's sleep and sweating out his surprise and aggression, he had more perspective.

With each post-jog squat, lunge, and push-up, he reminded himself that Rhiannon had warned him about the Hive's unorthodoxy before he'd Devoted. Plus, he knew she relied on him. *As long as everyone centers on the Queen, does it matter whether they're male or female? Dyfed-born or offworlder? Druidic or Catholic?*

This was a good thing really. If Rhiannon could accept a woman, she could definitely accept *him*.

He'd have to try interacting with Alan again. They were the odd ones. They'd truly come for *Rhiannon*, working to build their lives around her, where the others leaned on pre-established friendships. Though his last talk with Alan hadn't gone so well. The man had been rude... but he'd offered Luciano his sandwich.

Speakers in the corridor crackled to life. "We're going to the station in half an hour." His Queen's voice echoed through the hollow halls. "Anyone who wants to see the Beltane fires or pick up some furniture should meet me at the airlock."

Luciano wasn't sure about the outing. On the one hand, he wanted to spend time with his Hive mates— especially his Queen—and to get supplies for Medical. On the other hand, Beltane.

The sweat cooled on his body and made his skin prickle with bumps, but his face was a brazier. That was just the exercise talking, not any reluctance. Still, Beltane. *When Christian priests used to eat the meat from pagan sacrifices on Earth, God didn't mind, right? As long as they didn't believe in the barbaric deities, they were safe.* Luciano couldn't remember where he'd heard that.

How could he tell his Hive he didn't want to do this one thing with them? He wanted to share their lives and their worries, yes, but not this aspect of their culture. He wasn't a druid. He didn't want to be.

God willing, they wouldn't mind.

Back in his room, he threw on the least interesting clothes he owned, hoping to go unnoticed by the Beltane revelers. He felt sloppy in an old brown tunic and worn green trousers that were too short to tuck into his everyday boots. *Choke on that, druids. I won't primp for your pagan holidays.* No one would think he'd dressed up for whatever god this festival honored.

When he arrived at the airlock, he found his whole Hive. All of them had dressed down. *Now it looks like I'm celebrating in the same way they are.* Rhiannon was resplendent as always in a high-collared black tunic he recognized as three years out of style. The black made her dark hair glow. The others were just as nondescript as himself in brown, brown, and more brown. Even Gavin had gone for local traditional garb. *Maybe his flamboyant outfit last night wasn't normal?*

"*Dilyn fi,*" Rhiannon said. Everyone fell in behind her as she led the way. Luciano followed as well. He'd just pretend he spoke Cymraeg today. His mother would be so proud that he'd found a proper Welsh Hive. *If only they'd remember that my second language is Italian!*

He staggered under stifling heat the moment they left the docking spoke. Burnt oat smoke attacked his nose. Bells rang nonstop.

"Do you really need me today?" he asked his companions, more than ready to turn back around and keep an eye on the *Cauldron*.

No one acknowledged the question.

Luciano trudged along with his Hive, largely tuning out their happy chatter. He heard enough to know that Rhiannon and Alan had devolved into some sort of Cymraeg poetry recital.

The burnt oats filled his lungs. He gasped for breath. His eyes watered, but he refused to lag behind and rub at them. Luciano lengthened his stride. If he was going to be here, he was going to keep up with everyone. He was going to bond with his Hive today, even if the smoke blinded him.

He longed for the ship's cool emptiness. Even the pilot house would be refreshing after the heat of Beltane fires that he had yet to see. Maybe the station just raised the temperature for their revelry. Over the bells—the incessant bells!—a recorded message added to the din. It finished up whatever it was saying. *In Cymraeg, of course.* Luciano didn't understand it and didn't care to.

If his eyes watered, it was just the smoke and the heat.

"Luciano!" That was Gavin's high voice, filling the air around them with panic.

Then Luciano was on the ground, where the smoke didn't sting his eyes as much. The hard floors knocked his bones and offered bruises to his skin. He could breathe easier now, free of the oat and the heat, smothered instead by Gavin's chest and the pervasive sweet scent of candied citrus. *I won't be manhandled!* He pushed Gavin away, missing the candy smell immediately. "What the Hell?"

Luciano bounced to his feet, ready to punch his Hive mate for the unnecessary tackle. Gavin just shrugged and gestured to the empty air, cocking his head pointedly.

I'll knock that pointy chin right into the wall.

Luciano paused in his murderous peregrination when he heard the recorded message, now in English. "Fire hazard. Keep clear when lights are blinking."

He squinted through the thick air. He'd been standing directly next to a blinking light when Gavin tackled him. His anger ran out like pasta water through a sieve. "Thanks," he said.

***

When they finally reached the main concourse, Luciano detached himself from the others. They were easy to persuade. "You go ahead," he said. "Buy me an oat cake while I deal with the shopping."

The Quartermaster's office was empty except for a woman behind the counter. She had a pad in front of her, and an older model sat on the customer side. The evidence of heavy items' transportation scuffed the floors. The brightly lit walls showcased posters for *The Latest in Compression Socks* or *Forty Days of Meals in One Tiny Package*.

Luciano had a necessities list on his own pad. He reveled in the office-shop's quiet calm and plugged into the system, pulling up the order numbers for the things everyone wanted.

Gwyn flashed him a message. *Don't forget nitrogen-enhanced soil.*

Victor followed up immediately after. *Toothbrushes please!*

He waited a few moments, but nothing more came. They'd forgotten about him, about errands. *Or maybe they already added things to the list and are having a good time... without you.*

"Ahem," he said, wanting the woman's attention.

"Joyful Beltane," she said automatically. She didn't sound very joyful. She also didn't look up from her pad. "Buy something or get out."

Luciano bounced on his toes. *Finally! Someone as disenchanted with the holiday as I am!* "Can you complete this order please? Also, my life sciences person said something about nitro-soil. Oh, and I need sheets! But I can't figure out the system."

She still didn't look at him, but his order form had made it to her pad, so that was all for the best. "Sure, I've got a good soil mixture. What kind of sheets do you want?"

Of course there was more than one sheet type. "Whatever's standard."

The woman sighed. It was an impressive sigh, brimming with annoyance and superiority at once. "What class of ship do you have?"

They come in classes? "Ahm..."

She sighed even louder and turned her back to him, taking the pad with her. She could use it just as well facing him or the wall, so it was clearly a symbolic gesture. "Which ship is it? I can look you up."

Oh. "That's great!" He tried to sound excited and happy. He didn't want to alienate the Quartermaster even further. "I'm with the *Ceridwen's Cauldron*."

That got her attention. She whirled on him, mouth drawn down in a furious triangle. "You are much too young for that crew. I know Queen-Captain Ceridwen personally, and she will not be pleased." She held up her pad, screen facing him so he could watch as she deliberately deleted his order. "I should've known from your accent. No prank playing on my station, miner's child. Now get out!"

And here I thought my accent wouldn't matter anymore now that I'd joined a Hive. "You don't understand. The ship's under new management, and we don't have anything."

She started humming, and Luciano knew she wasn't going to listen. He'd failed to do this simple thing for his Hive. Now he had to find them, in shame, and participate in their bizarre druidic rituals. He flashed Rhiannon a message.

She immediately replied: *STAY THERE.*

She'd been watching her pad, even during some culturally significant revelry. She thought he was more important than the holiday party with the others!

He'd never disobey a direct command. He waited at the door.

In moments, his Queen stood before him, her hair frizzing like a halo around her head.

"Don't worry about a thing, Luciano." Her voice was the warm breath of life, speaking his name in a dark, I'm-in-control voice. "Take me to see the Quartermaster."

Together they approached the counter. As before, the woman didn't look up, preferring to work with her pad. "I told you to get out of here, kid. Don't make me call spacedock security."

"Hmmm." Mocking observation filled Rhiannon's tone. "I do see your problem, Luciano." She elongated her vowels in all the right places to give her a classical Welsh lilt.

The woman's head snapped up at that tone. She had a real customer to deal with, a high class one. "Oh, um. Joyful Beltane?"

Rhiannon smirked, and Luciano loved her a little more in that moment. "*Beltane Llawen.*"

For once, he didn't mind the Welsh. It unnerved the annoying woman further.

"Now please tell me why my ship can't have provisions and explain why you've Sent My Devoted Away." She emphasized her displeasure with those last words.

The Quartermaster's shoulders relaxed. She mirrored Rhiannon's smirk. "Him? Really?" She tapped an impatient finger on the counter. "If you want to play games, kid, you need better accomplices than miner's children from Dyfed3. *Nuova*, they call it. No one will ever believe he's a real Devoted."

Rhiannon looked the woman directly in the eyes and leaned forward like a predator. The Quartermaster couldn't look away, didn't move under her gaze. "Is that so?" Still maintaining eye contact, she hooked her pad to the Quartermaster's with an actual cable.

The woman's pad pinged, but she didn't look down. His Queen's vicious smile threatened to rend flesh from bone, if she moved without permission. The other woman couldn't know that Rhiannon was so small and gentle.

"Am I a Queen now?" Rhiannon asked, breaking her stare and letting the Quartermaster look to her pad.

The woman breathed out an oath. She dropped her head in submission rather than disinterest this time. "My apologies, Queen-Commander Ceridwen. I wasn't aware the ship had changed hands."

Rhiannon waved her fingers dismissively. "Get my Devoted whatever he wants. Add it to the ship's credit account." She turned her back on the Quartermaster, insult and change of topic. To Luciano she said, "Oh, here. I brought you an oat cake."

**

When Luciano went to bed that night, he stretched out on crisp blue sheets. He'd taken three showers to get rid of the smell of burnt oat and singed hair. His muscles ached from jumping through shimmering air—the space-dock's equivalent of a Beltane fire—holding hands with Rhiannon on one side and Gavin on the other.

This Hive thing was really going to work out.

CHAPTER ELEVEN

The Passenger

Saint Christopher, please bless our travels. Don't let me mess this up.

Today, they'd disengage from the spaceport and head out on their own. Luciano had to get the ship safely from one place to the next.

He took a brief shower, the last one with spaceport water, and dressed in his most fashionable brown loose trousers, tucked into his calf-high boots, and a bright orange tunic that proclaimed his allegiance to Dyfed Mining Co. He definitely looked good. When Rhiannon saw him this morning, she'd be amazed by the improvements in his attitude and his clothing.

Without doubt, she'd comment on his positivity. Maybe her eyes would linger on his emblazoned chest. He might be shorter than the other men in her Hive, but he was a hell of a lot more muscular.

"All hands, all hands." Rhiannon's voice came over the PA. Today, at least, she tried to warn them all to listen before getting to the meat of the message. The previous day's announcement about heading into the concourse for Beltane had been more abrupt. "Let's head down to the dining area. I'll bring our new passenger to meet you. See you there!"

It wasn't the most professional sounding address, but the friendliness made Luciano smile. He bounced on his toes and took off running.

His toothy smile faded when he entered the dining hall and saw his compatriots. Alan and Gwyn hadn't bothered to show up. Victor leaned on the metal table, looking bored. At least Gavin had a positive demeanor, though that came from dreamy wistfulness as he gazed off into nothing.

"Good morning?" Luciano tried.

"Definitely good," Gavin agreed, joining the here and now. "If we weren't here, we'd be in school."

Luciano smiled, though his teeth stayed firmly under his lips for it. He'd never understood what people had against school days. After working so hard to make it to Dyfed from Nuova, he'd show up even if he had to drag a priest saying Last Rites behind him. "Should only be about second period."

Showing some life, Victor paced next to the table. His bony frame made him seem small, even though he was the tallest person on the ship. Luciano's mother would have called him *spindle shank.*

"No one knows to look for us yet." Victor watched the door like a demon at the entrance to Hell, expecting escape with the next damned soul's arrival. "This passenger needs to get here so we can get out."

Sharp clicks, not quite in syncopated time, interfered with Victor's staccato rhythm. Gavin grabbed his friend's sleeve, dragging him back to form a miniature receiving line. Luciano wished he'd got Victor to stand straight too, instead of slouching, but that didn't matter.

Luciano was facing his taller crewmates when the door slid open and Rhiannon entered the dining hall. He tried to catch her gaze, to see if she noticed his presence and his outfit, but her eyes flitted over the room, taking in nothing.

She preceded a middle aged, portly man with ash-brown hair who was taller than Luciano, but definitely shorter than the other two present. The man used his long nose to full effect, measuring the three Devoted against it and finding them wanting.

Having dismissed the boys as beneath him, the man turned his back on the room and addressed Rhiannon.

"Young lady," he began.

How dare he! She was a Queen, *his* Queen, and should be spoken to with respect. Youth or not, any Queen of Dyfed outranked the officious buggers who stalled out in middling politic. Why, Luciano wouldn't be surprised to hear the man hadn't been allowed to Devote. He could easily be one of the masses that weren't important enough, smart enough, *talented* enough, to join a Hive. A real Hive member would be significantly higher up in government.

"I am appalled. Appalled!" The man put his arm around Rhiannon's shoulders.

Luciano growled. The man didn't notice this reaction to the over-familiarity, but Victor and Gavin gave him panicked looks. Victor and Gavin! Why weren't they upset at this treatment? What kind of Hive was this, anyway?

"I've been couriered on the *Ceridwen's Cauldron* before, under the previous crew. I knew the ship had changed hands, that it had become a training ship. But such disrepair in so short a time? The shabby floors clank when you walk. And you brought me to the mess hall in order to meet more children? Children! Are there any adults on this ship?"

Luciano leapt towards the man's back. He'd pull that offending arm off his Queen's inviolate person. She shouldn't be subjected to this. She shouldn't have to deal with such disrespect.

He never reached the man. Gavin tackled Luciano to the hard, cold floor just as the passenger and their Queen departed. The Devoted pair banged off it together, soft flesh and springy muscle.

Luciano hit the floor again on the bounce, the back of his head blooming with sensitivity.

"Fuck." *Please forgive me, Father, for I have sinned.* He lay still, breathing through the pain.

She hadn't even looked at him.

His eyes swam—just from the knock on the head—but he could see the fuzzy outline of a hand proffered. He took it and let Gavin pull him to his feet. Muscles screamed in his shoulder socket, and he swallowed against a wave of vertigo.

Gavin held his hand for a moment longer, helping him steady himself. "Sorry," Gavin said. "But we were supposed to make a good impression."

Victor snorted. "I don't think we succeeded."

Luciano extricated his hand. "Is this going to be a trend?" Twice now Gavin had knocked him over for his own good.

Gavin clapped Luciano on the shoulder. "We didn't kill our first passenger. That's a start!" He held up three fingers. "How many?"

Luciano shrugged. He saw the digits, no doubling or continued fuzziness. He'd be fine. Besides, Gavin was right about not attacking passengers, particularly passengers who could report their activities. No one wanted to get sent home with a black mark on his records for striking out too soon.

He needed to be up in the pilot house if this ship was going to go anywhere.

As he departed, Gavin called out. "We'll be in engineering if you need us."

The morning wasn't a total wash. They were getting along.

***

Thirty minutes later, he was alone in the pilot house. The chair was firm and unforgiving beneath him. It encased his legs in its implacable embrace and offered a hard surface to bang the back of his head against. The chair was probably designed for someone taller, or with their own padding.

He skimmed the relevant manual chapter one more time—*Even You Can Plot A Course Through A Crowded System*. The section's last words read, "Good luck." Was that a friendly encouragement or a disparaging remark on the skill of a pilot who needed to read this particular manual?

Regardless of the authors' intentions, the *Manual Pilot Manual* had helped. He'd correctly requested permission to release docking tethers. He'd acquired a position in the departure queue. He'd filed a flight plan from the spaceport above Dyfed to the diplomatic station on the system's edge. Hopefully, he'd even managed to keep them from looping through English space, but the border was shaky near the diplomatic station. God willing, whoever approved that flight plan had actually checked it.

A light on the pilot board blinked amber. He wasn't entirely sure what function that light mapped to, but his spot in the queue came any second. He didn't have time to check it.

Over unseen speakers, a tinny voice announced, "*Ceridwen's Cauldron, Ceridwen's Cauldron. You are in the middle of your flight zone. Please depart immediately or revise your stated plans.*"

Luciano jolted back in his chair, slamming his parietal bone against the headrest. Where was the communication response button again?

His hands ranged over the board in front of him, floating above it like jellyfish. As he followed the movements with his eyes, everything turned to a focused blur. He couldn't see the specific controls. The mass of lights was all he could see.

"Ceridwen's Cauldron, Ceridwen's Cauldron."

The message repeated again. A live person?

His manual wasn't on the board, but Luciano couldn't search for it now. He had to find the switch for something useful, for anything useful. It was right in front of him. It had to be. They'd designed the board so that everything immediate was right in front of him.

A button flashed. Luciano jammed it down with his finger till the sore digit protested. He had a moment to register that the button had been flashing green. Thank God.

He looked up from the board and saw the spaceport falling away. It sat in space like a friendly dog, tether-tails waving and not quite guarding the planet. That amber light could have been attached to a timer, or to communications, or to the spaceport tethers. He'd look it up later.

The *Manual Pilot Manual* skidded across the floor thanks to inertia.

The tinny voice returned briefly. *"Brigid guide you, Ceridwen's Cauldron. And don't cut it so close next time, eh?"*

Luciano would've replied, but he didn't know how. The spaceport glittered with the sun's light, a jewel on the planet's setting. It was getting smaller by the moment. "God be praised," he breathed.

He tore his eyes from the window and refocused them on the pilot board. Without the pressure, everything was much clearer. He could match up the bits and pieces with the directions and pictures in the *Manual Pilot Manual*. So, somewhere around here there should be... Aha!

He attended the distance read-out, poised to make the change from planetary thrusters to in-system drives. The numbers jumped, then jumped again. Master of the pilot house, he had this completely under control.

Just as the manual described, he flipped the protective case around the red-painted, thumb-sized toggle. He rested his right hand against it. His left hand went to the round dial that controlled gravity in the drive chambers. Switching between drives was tricky, the manual said, and should only be done under zero-gee conditions.

He breathed in, then out. He sucked and discarded air three times, as the town surgeon had demonstrated during his internship before leaving Nuova. You had to clear your mind and control your body before undertaking a delicate procedure.

Now! He turned the gravity dial and flipped the gear switch at the same time.

Nothing happened. No sudden acceleration slammed him back into the blasted headrest. No alarms rang out warning.

He'd have to try again.

Luciano looked out the window, needing to focus on something other than his failure inside the pilot house.

The spaceport wasn't there.

"Woohoo!" He laughed at his victory and punched the cabin's air at a diagonal. He'd done it.

More confident now, he made some quick course corrections. The steering was dead easy, just a matter of ensuring that current projections matched the flight plan. Making the flight plan had been the hard part.

After the quick check, he dismissed himself. The little ship could continue on without his direct supervision for a while. While it drove on its own, he'd visit with Rhiannon and get his much deserved praise for a smooth uncoupling.

He slipped the buckles that secured his legs to the chair and disengaged the three point harness on his chest. After giving picking up the *MPM* and giving it a fond pat, Luciano stood up.

And kept going.

Up and up, he went, until he bounced off the ceiling. God knew his head had taken more than its fair share of bumps today.

Great. I must have turned off gravity to the whole ship when I turned it off in the gear box.

He checked the gravity dial and nudged it in each direction. He gave it his most forbidding look. "I've turned you every which way now. Are you taking me for a spin?" He played with the dial some more to no avail.

For twenty minutes, he turned the knob, flipped through the manual, and pleaded with the gravity to just turn on already. He opened every possible drawer, looking for further buttons that might be marked *Gravity Savior*. He hadn't found such a button, but he had found (1) a packet of crisps and (2) the lockbox with the ship's single projectile weapon—for safety and security.

A beep informed him that someone was calling up to the pilot house. *Let's take a break from this fruitless searching.* When he recognized the caller, he groaned.

Their politician passenger blinked beady eyes and declared in strident tones, "You will put me through to your captain at once, young man. This is unacceptable. Unacceptable!"

I can make it worse. Luciano figured he shouldn't bait the passenger. "I'm terribly sorry for any inconvenience. Commander Ceridwen isn't here at the moment. May I take a message?"

The politician's face flushed crimson, starting at his mouth. "Now, look here, young man!" He leaned in, peering intently at the panels behind Luciano. "Are *you* the pilot?"

Luciano pasted on his blandest smile. He didn't even grit his teeth. "Yes. How can I help you?"

"Help me? How can you help me?" The incredulity in the passenger's voice could have been better disguised. Though that probably wasn't the point. "When was the last time your pilot's license was updated? I plan to write a strongly worded letter to your issuing institution, young man!" He was panting.

The institution of Read-The-Manual University will be happy to ignore your complaints, sir.

"You do that," he drawled.

The passenger's breathing sped up into a frothy puffing. "Is this how you treat all official envoys?"

Luciano shrugged, enjoying the way it made the man's eyes even wilder. "You're my first."

"First? First!" The man spluttered for a few moments before cutting the connection on his end.

Luciano bet the passenger would turn puce when he looked for his pilot's license. Still, it was good that he'd called. It had reminded Luciano that he could call for help too. *This Hive may have zero pilots, but it has three engineers!* One of them should be able to do something about this unfortunate gravity situation, or at least absolve Luciano's guilt over causing it.

Unfortunately, when he tried calling down to said engineers—well, two CreaTechs and one *busy busy give me a few minutes*—Victor and Gavin were totally lost.

Victor shrugged his ignorance and disinterest. Gavin, at least, moved halfway out of the picture to hunch over a console that might be related to the problem.

"I think I can find a directory," he mumbled around a Tribute he'd shoved in his mouth. He never finished that thought, or else it only made sense to the other two near him, because Luciano stayed on the line waiting while Gavin wandered off.

"Oh, for the beauty of the universe!" Alan's deeply resonant and very annoyed voice reminded Luciano of his mother's whenever he and his sister frustrated her common sense.

Luciano's mouth stretched in a silent laugh, and Alan's face filled his screen. It was a roundish face with a too wide nose, what his mother would call *kissable lips*, and topped by messy brown hair that looked like it needed a trim, especially since its owner kept flipping it out of his eyes. His skin, almost dark enough to compete with Luciano's own for the honor of *least pale Hive member*, had a sickly grey cast from hermitage.

"Look," Alan said. He pointed a finger at the screen as though Luciano might not be aware he had been addressed. "Stay where you are. I'll be up in a few minutes to see what I can do."

"I'll be here."

And then engineering cut the connection.

Luciano fiddled with the drive's gravity-knob some more, but didn't want to touch anything else in case it only made things worse. He picked up the manual again and hunted through the index. There had to be something in there about drive switching and unresolved gravity.

The chronometer said he'd gotten off with engineering ten minutes ago.

He read about *Basic Procedures for Morons*. He thought he'd checked that section thoroughly, but he'd hate to find out that the problem lay in the *Morons* section.

The next chronometer check said he'd gotten off with

engineering seventeen minutes ago. Apparently, Alan intended to take his sweet time getting up to the pilot house.

It's not like the passenger called up here or anything. We don't need to hurry.

At twenty-five minutes, as Luciano was contemplating calling down again, Alan floated upwards through the floor entrance. He'd bypassed the ladder, simply flying into the pilot house. He managed not to hit his head on the ceiling by stopping himself with an upraised hand.

The supposed genius wore old clothes—worn twill leggings and the form-fitting sleeves you saw in lab workers so their tunics didn't knock into anything. Luciano flattened himself against a wall when Alan sailed directly to the pilot board, carrying the scent of burnt circuitry into the little cocoon.

The engineer felt around the pilot board's stem like a blind man giving it a hug until he found a panel to pop off. From there, he did *something* that inspired a little happy puff of *ooh*. Then he consulted his pad, which now sported scrolling data. It looked like he'd found the directory that Gavin had claimed to be hunting for, if Luciano were interpreting correctly.

"That's just disturbing," Alan said. Three ridges formed on his forehead while he tapped at his pad a bit more.

"What is?" Luciano knew better than to interrupt a specialist, but that sounded dire.

Alan flipped his pad to show Luciano whatever he'd found, but the lines didn't inform the doctor-cum-pilot much. "See here? The automatic systems should have taken care of the gravity when they engaged the in-system drive. I hate to imagine what other defects might crop up."

That was news. "We have automatics? What else do they do?"

Alan didn't look up from his pad, still tapping away, but his fingers slowed for a moment while he digested information. When he spoke, his voice held that brand of horrified patience Luciano's mother's did whenever she'd learned that he had spirited himself away to play in the abandoned mineshafts as a child. "You've been flying *manually*? What are you doing for course corrections?"

The course corrections weren't all that hard, not compared to plotting the course the first time. "I just check our position against where I told the spaceport we'd be at a given time. Then do all my vector mapping to push us the right way. Is there an automatic system for that too?"

Now Alan did look up with all the manic intensity of a man about to bestow seven hundred kisses. "Can I see your flight plan?"

Luciano shrugged. "Sure." He pulled the map up on the main pilot board and handed the other boy the pad on which he'd worked out all the calculations.

Alan tried his own equations and variations on the same problems using the constraints that Luciano had provided—such as English space's current borders. His eyebrows rose. He abandoned his pad to do something with Luciano's proffered one.

"That's really tidy," Alan finally said.

"Thanks. Don't suppose you have any pointers?"

Alan shook his head. "Nope. I couldn't have done any better, and I spend my spare time on tensor physics." He handed Luciano's pad back. "But I can help you with the gravity problem. I've slaved the drive system automatics into this macro here." He pointed to a button marked *Auto Drive.* "Just be sure to engage this whenever you make a switch."

Luciano clapped his new friend on the shoulder, and they both went sailing in opposite directions. This time, he put out a hand to protect himself from the bulkhead. They bounced off the walls and came together in the middle, clasping hands so as not to go flying off again. The adrenaline and the relief bubbled in him like a well treated with Hydrolyze.

Luciano's laughter set off Alan's. They rested against each other in the small room, inhaling each other's mirth until the joy settled down to a contented simmer.

Calmer now, they prepared to set things to rights. They found the application that let them send an audio-only message ship-wide. As pilot, Luciano made the announcement. "Everyone please get in contact with the floor. We might be about to regain a sense of up and down."

As he spoke, Alan entered and executed the command into his pad, still linked with the pilot board.

Luciano's body settled into place, his muscles taking over once again to compensate for his body's weight. He felt the floor pressing into his boots, and relaxed his arms to the sides, helped along by unnatural nature. "Let's not mess with any other automatic systems just

114

yet," he said. "We can pick up a book or three next time we hook up to some planet's intranet."

Alan nodded his breathless agreement. They both pretended they weren't worried. If they'd missed this automatic system, what else might exist?

CHAPTER TWELVE

Studying and Skiving

Rhiannon needed more data. Dyfed had decades of data on interpersonal interactions, ship owning, and how to be a responsible Queen or Commander. All laid out and organized into beautifully sensible and chronological chunks by teams of Analysts and Historians.

Rhiannon just needed access. And a few months to read it all. She could read fast, right? No matter what she'd done to the Test, she was a Perceiver by nature.

Perceivers: no, we're not clairvoyant, just really good at drawing conclusions.

But you couldn't draw an accurate conclusion if you didn't have anything to base it on.

Her pad, synched to the ship's network, beeped and flashed its light. For a moment, she considered ignoring the message request, staying away from the others till she was ready. She had so much to do, so much to try and learn from half-mentioned ideas and unstated facts.

Oh, who was she kidding? She'd set herself an impossible task, and any distraction was a good one. Gwyn's oval face with its long, skinny nose filled Rhiannon's tiny pad screen. *Definitely a good distraction.* "You look like Pwyll after slogging through Annwyn's forests," Gwyn said.

Rhiannon's hand came up to smooth her hair. She had a terrible tendency to scrunch it up till it got all shandi-vang whenever she got frustrated or upset.

"You want to come braid this mess?" she asked.

"That's why I called." Gwyn turned the pad so that Rhiannon could see the bed in her room, covered in clothes, a sewing kit, and other colorful goodies. "No one's seen you in ages, my dear. You need a break."

Yes. The thought was like a sigh in the back of her mind, breathing cool air on her overheated brain. Hearing someone else say it made it acceptable. She had permission to step away from this fruitless hunt for information.

"Consider it done," Rhiannon said. "I'm coming over."

In bare moments, she was curled on Gwyn's flannel blankets and rolling paint onto her ragged fingernails. The other girl situated herself on the floor, a hem press beside her, needle in hand for little details. Gwyn pressed and tucked, sliding folded material into the hemming machine next to her, letting it do most of the work.

Their calm activities were matched by a conversation that had nothing to do with their situation. Nothing radical or unknown. Gwyn asked, "Do you remember that crush you had on that university guy in that restaurant? Did you ever do anything about it?"

Rhiannon giggled, thinking about the tall stranger working his way through a university experience that the state didn't provide. She'd admired his ambition. Maybe he wasn't Devoted material, but he'd been hard working and handsome. His raven-black hair and wire-sharp nose had made him look old and young all at once.

"Nn-mm," she denied. "What would I have said? And what if he'd turned out to be icky in reality?" Her voice went high-pitched on *icky* and stayed there for the rest of the sentence. Now that she didn't have to sound commanding, she could speak in any register she wanted.

Gwyn pulled her third tunic out of the hem press and *tsk*ed at its edge. She licked a thread and wended it through the needle. "When we go back, you can see if he's still there. After all, you'll have your whole Hive behind you. If he turned out to be *icky* we could all console you."

Gwyn didn't say *if we go back*. She said *when*.

Rhiannon wasn't going to think about that right now. No, she was going to think about hot boys she could have crushes on. The stranger in the restaurant was *safe*, not like the Devoted in her Hive. Especially because he wasn't here.

Here the men all worked for her approval. They cared about her well-being, but she couldn't approach them. Wouldn't want to approach them. They weren't for her. And not just because it'd play merry havoc with the Hive dynamics.

They weren't what she wanted, what she could let herself want. They needed her too much. She didn't want that kind of pressure in a relationship. Someday she'd meet someone who could survive without her. Someone who could be a whole person on his own. Someone who could love her without any ulterior motives.

In another world, maybe Gavin, for all his melodrama. And she knew that Luciano had an inappropriate level of feeling, but she would never shame him by acknowledging it.

Back home, back when they were best friends and didn't have a Hive to consider, Rhiannon would've told Gwyn about Luciano's growing feelings, but now she couldn't. Even here, in this girly-gossip zone, duty encroached.

Rhiannon finished rolling the rose petal paint onto her pinky. It wasn't really her shade, but it was what Gwyn had on hand. "I have to go," Rhiannon said. "Lots to do. You know how it is."

Gwyn's perfectly pink lips formed a concerned frown. "But I haven't even braided your hair yet." The tunics she'd worked on looked like a whole new wardrobe—asymmetrical hems where they'd originally been straight, wrap waists where there'd once been cardigans.

Rhiannon had to get out of here, out of this safe zone where Hives and leadership and lack of data didn't exist. Tears pricked the corners of her eyes. This scene Gwyn had set, it was too comfortable, too gentle and sweet. It only reminded her how unsettling the real world was.

Gwyn climbed onto the bed behind her and finger-combed her frizzing hair. "Just relax and let me. Please?"

The digits curled and tangled like a trap. Rhiannon slumped backwards into her friend's hands. Gwyn wouldn't hurt her, not really. "I suppose I can stay a few minutes."

Gwyn sectioned the crown, and Rhiannon felt the rhythmic tugs of a French braid-in-progress. "Do you think Victor's getting bored of me?"

What? Rhiannon tried to spin and see the other girl, to read her face. "What?"

Gwyn pulled her back into position. "Don't move." She briefly massaged the area she'd abused. "It's just… He's been avoiding me, I think."

Rhiannon looked down at her pink nails. The pastel made her feel weak. "Well, you *have* been hiding from the passenger. It's more like you're avoiding all the major areas of the ship, I think. While Victor's spending his time in them."

Gwyn dropped the hair in her hands and finger-combed it out again. She re-sectioned and started over. "Well, if you haven't seen more of him either…"

I didn't say that. But it was true. Gwyn had been hiding from the passenger, and Rhiannon had been staying in her room. Until she'd read up enough on leadership. "He hasn't even Devoted to me, you know. Not really."

Gwyn gasped and buried her fingers in Rhiannon's hair, heedless of the progress of her braiding.

Rhiannon smiled, though Gwyn couldn't see it.

I thought that might be it. At least she knew how to read her best friend. That was something. She continued, "He loves you. He started this whole scheme for you. Do you really think he'd throw you over for *me?*"

Rhiannon only knew Victor through Gwyn, and they'd never liked each other much. In some ways, it was like Gwyn was the Queen, and Victor and Rhiannon were her Devoted. Their love of Gwyn pulled them together and made them get along. Someday, the three of them might act like a family.

More likely, though, Victor and Gwyn would melt away from her. They'd set up their own happy life. Victor would be more *Gwyn's lover* than *Rhiannon's Devoted,* and Rhiannon's faux-Hive would fall apart.

Everyone left eventually.

She had to figure out this leadership thing. Then she'd know how to keep them all together.

Gwyn finished up the braid and tied it off with a scrap of fabric she'd cut from a tunic during her wardrobe re-vamp. "There you go."

Rhiannon's quarters called to her. She had research to do. "I'll see you later."

Gwyn hugged her from behind. Rhiannon didn't turn around to return it. She simply headed out, mind already reviewing what she'd read so far.

CHAPTER THIRTEEN

Bleak Romantic Prospects

Two days after the incident with the gravity, Victor was taking as much time as he could at Gwyn's door as he exited. He didn't want to leave her. *Gods, if only I could stay by her side forever!* But she needed to hide away while they had a passenger. She couldn't be seen.

He slammed an open palm into the doorframe, relishing the sting. It was so unfair! They'd left Dyfed so that they wouldn't have to hide their love, but Dyfed followed them wherever they went.

No. He wouldn't complicate this leave-taking with such thoughts. He'd concentrate on other things. Like on Gwyn's room. Her room was the homiest place he'd been on the ship so far, warm with blankets and decorated with family photos and art that her brother had made before getting shipped off for his little sister's own good.

She cares so much about the people in her life, knows how to make a place feel like a home. How lucky I am that she turns that care onto me.

He leaned against the frame, his muscles relaxed and his whole being focused on his love. She finished puttering about and finally joined him at the door.

"You'll be careful?" The admonishment came out a question. "When you practice stage combat with Gavin? It may be just a hobby and for show, but it's still dangerous."

How sweet that she worries for me! His absent father had never looked after him so well, and his mother doted more on his little sister.

We'll take care of each other. Forever.

He stepped away from the wall and closed the distance between them. Only slightly shorter, she fit perfectly inside his stance. He tried to wrap his presence around her when they stood chest to chest.

"It's only my second lesson," he reassured her. He raised a hand to card through the white-blond strands above her left ear. "When I'm a master of the quarterstaff, you'll wish you'd come along."

It was the closest he'd gotten to inviting her to join him in the sessions. When she didn't pick up on it, his stomach loosened from pent-up anxiety. She'd change the dynamic just by being there. Instead of being about his body and the movement, it would be about protecting Gwyn or looking good in her eyes. He couldn't handle that right now. When Gavin had let him try out the sport the day before, Victor had immediately felt... purposeful. And *that* for the first time since leaving the spaceport.

Truth was, he was starting to doubt his abilities and interests as a CreaTech. *Wouldn't some Test computer somewhere be scared for its circuits to learn that!* And while he waited for inspiration, he saw Gavin tinkering with little machines and fixing tanks with nothing more than his eyes and a welder. And he saw Alan doing incomprehensible gobbledygook with equations and computers that didn't seem to be affected one way or the other by his work.

And he saw Gavin exclaiming over Alan's imperceptible-to-Victor changes, impressed. Maybe that was the worst part.

The other two did their own things—without needing to be told *hey, make this* or *hey, fix that*—but they also consulted each other. They weren't best buddies; Gavin would never give Alan stage combat lessons. Still, they respected each other as engineers. Alan held things when Gavin needed extra hands. Gavin checked Alan's math.

And what does Victor do? Nothing, that's what. Gods, why can't I take control of something? I should probably talk with the Commander and ask her to assign me a project. The others didn't seem all that much better than me when we left Dyfed, but now...

He pushed the unworthy thoughts away and breathed in Gwyn's warmth and love. It spread through his blood, circulating through his body and making him a stronger, better man. He stroked her pale skin under his fingers, its porcelain texture so different from his own. She made a little *mewl*, and his ardor heated.

"Can't leave without a good-bye kiss," he said playfully.

She tilted her head, teasing and compliant at once. His nerves exploded when their lips touched. She was hot, cold, prickly, smooth, savory, sweet. One touch, mouth to mouth, and he lost himself in the wonder. Kissing his girl-friend would never get old.

They broke apart, reconnected, foreheads pressed to-gether. He opened his eyes—and when had he closed them?—and felt the warm connection flowing from her hazel orbs into his own muddy brown ones. He exhaled, unable to contain love's fires consuming the oxygen inside.

A rude voice interrupted their peace. "How touching."

Victor spun to face the voice, protecting Gwyn with his body. "I, uh..." He had nothing to say. No words to make the politician un-witness a female non-Queen onsite.

"Well?" The politician prodded ungently. He arched eyebrows in false interest. "Aren't you going to invite me inside?"

They couldn't run away. Mute, the lovers backed into Gwyn's cozy room, letting the interloper follow. Victor tried to put some distance between Gwyn and the man, shooing her to sit on the bed. The politician cast an un-caring eye over the wall art.

"Can we help you?" Victor was pleased his voice didn't shake. Maybe he'd get lucky and the man wouldn't care about a young woman traveling with a newly formed Hive. Maybe the man would be super-progressive? *Yeah,*

125

and Lleu's mother named him on purpose. When you didn't believe your own hopeful lies, you knew you were in trouble.

The politician ran fingers over Gwyn's photographs, leaving behind smears of finger oil. "Does your captain know about this?" His voice was light, conversational.

Victor wasn't fooled by the casualness. The older man stood tall; he knew he was in control.

Gwyn answered in her high, sweet voice. "Of course she does."

The man speared Gwyn with such a condescendingly disdainful look that Victor felt ashamed for the first time since starting this scheme. "Young lady, do not interrupt me!" A smile played at the corners of his lips, not quite escaping. *He's enjoying this!*

Victor didn't point out that she'd only been answering his question.

The man laced his fingers and brought them up until the knuckles rapped against his nose. His attention shifted away from Gwyn and back to Victor. "And what do you get out of this?" He said *this* like a dead rat dropped from his lips with the word, and he gestured to the room at large. "*What* is worth being unfaithful to your Queen?"

It wasn't worth pointing out that Rhiannon had decided to identify as a Commander. That fact didn't matter. Because the man was right. Victor's Devotion to his Queen had been compromised, and for what? He hadn't even managed to make his temporary, not good enough, horribly conditional vows. Somehow, he hadn't made the time.

He should be the envy of every Devoted his age anywhere in the Welsh system. He had a beautiful, smart Queen who trusted him so much that she let him keep his girlfriend.

And Victor repaid that trust with a hollow, ashen Devotion. If he couldn't Devote to this Queenly marvel, what was he? If his goal wasn't to be a perfect Devoted and CreaTech, what had been the point of his life until this point, all that schooling and excelling? But if he couldn't love his Gwyn with all his heart and soul, then what Devotion could he ever offer to anyone? He'd neither sworn his allegiance to Rhiannon nor given up on the whole system for his girlfriend's sake.

Gods, Victor thought, *I've been gifted with two marvelous situations, and I'm not giving either of them the care and attention they deserve.*

While Victor had fallen into his mental recriminations, the interloper had begun pacing. Now he rounded on Gwyn. "And you! What do you see in this unfaithful, worthless specimen?" He jabbed in Victor's direction. "Either you're ruining his life by holding him back or else he's not a good choice for a beautiful, smart young woman like yourself." He paused to let Gwyn think that over, then snapped, "Well? Which is it?"

Victor's eyes flew to his love, watching closely for any reaction. She flinched, though from the words or their delivery he couldn't tell. Victor pulled on his tunic's hem, his ragged nails catching in the weave and scratching red lines into the overheated flesh underneath.

She won't let this bastard convince her that she should leave me, right? Not even if he promises her a perfect life without me?

"We'll be fine," Victor snarled at the politician. "We're in love. Our Queen is secure enough in her place. Gwyn isn't planning to stray and become a disruption." More quietly, he repeated, "We'll be fine."

We can live among the stars where no one knows about my love and wants to take her away.

The man lifted a sardonic eyebrow. "Actually, my boy, you won't be fine unless I say so."

So casually, too casually for a man destroying lives, the politician continued. "I could simply mention this to the right people back home. You'd be wanted criminals. Wanted for lying, for stealing this ship and destroying a Hive's potential. Your careers and prospects would fade away. Oh, you could try to pass it off as youthful indiscretion, but that would probably only work for your lucky Queen. After all, we need Queens more than we need whatever *you* might do for the world." He spread his hands, palms up, as if benevolently encompassing that hypothetical world.

Victor's insides flash-fried. He stayed perfectly still, a crisped soul, and listened as the man pronounced his judgment. A trickle of sweat worked its way down Victor's forehead and over his nose. It plopped without opposition on his shirt.

But the passenger said nothing more. The man's hands trembled. He snarled at them, a wordless, vicious

128

sound. With that odd action—*isn't he the one in control?*—the man let himself out.

Gwyn sat on the bed, head bowed, expression hidden by the curtain of her long hair. But he heard her when she said, "We need to tell Rhi. She'll know what to do."

Victor shook his head in negation, even though she couldn't see him from inside her self-made cave. "No. I was already going to see Gavin. Let's talk with him first."

This time they didn't kiss at her door. Victor wondered if they'd ever kiss again.

Meanwhile, Back on Dyfed

Queen Olivia, the former Captain Ceridwen, ambled through a covered market in Machynlleth, the capital city, enveloped by her Devoted entourage. After so long shipboard, where the most spacious room could only contain twelve people, the planetside market rang with strangers shouting joys and mercantile desires. At least she was protected from the worst ignominies. How much worse this must be for her Devoted, getting jostled by the unknown locals as they shielded her.

Today she intended to purchase some foodstuffs and maybe a rug for their temporary abode, the small house provided by the government.

"After over a hundred years of service and your instrumental efforts towards opening up the in-system spacelanes during the dangerous years of exploration, it's the least we can do," the Minister for Commerce's representative had said. And good thing too, because Olivia had never gotten around to forming plans for her return to Dyfed. That had always seemed so far away. Without the largesse, her Hive might have been homeless, at least for these first few weeks. They had the money, but not the connections, not yet.

As a single unit her Hive shuffled away from a gaggle of teenagers and into the mostly empty deli-café. Olivia's Devoted looked old and weary, something she'd never seen in them before. Their shoulders rode low, and their mouths frowned so deeply. She couldn't bear to send them back out to brave the covered market again. Not yet.

"Why don't we sit and have a spot of tea?" she suggested.

In no time, her men had pushed together a few tables and slumped down into chairs, warming cold hands around ceramic mugs.

"Don't worry, boys." She tried to cheer them up. "We'll be used to this life again in no time. Why, I bet half of you will enjoy crowds, and the other half will rediscover delight in the outdoors."

Paul, the favorite she could never admit to having, rested his space-pale, blue-veined hand against her own. Perhaps now she could request that her Hive vote to allow her a romantic companion. She'd pick Paul if she could.

"I'm looking forward to getting a tan," he gamely rallied. A chorus of ayes greeted that suggestion.

A throat cleared behind her. "Queen Olivia Jones?"

Her Devoted stood to face this potential threat, but Olivia remained in her seat with her back to the newcomer. She was a *Queen*. Anyone who wished an audience would come to her. She might not stand on the formality of crowns and gowns, but she'd certainly not lower herself to interacting on a commoner's level. She remembered the days when the then-precarious Queen and Devoted system couldn't afford any slips.

Her men parted and allowed the stranger to kneel at her feet. When he straightened without permission, she had to look up at him. *Such arrogance!*

"Who comes before us?" she asked with cold disdain. He would acknowledge her status or she would ignore him utterly.

"Your ladyship." He averted his eyes respectfully. "I'm Jay Rogers from the Hive Relations Office. May I enquire whether you are the Queen Olivia who recently entered into a contract with Minister Llewellyn?"

Well, that was much more polite. "Yes, you may. And yes, I am. A bit of an insect, isn't he? What's he done?"

"I'm afraid I need to ask you some questions." Jay turned, as though expecting her to follow him from the little deli-café with its delightful tea and morsels. Without so much as a *please* or an *at your will.*

"We spoke with him only briefly," she informed him from her seat. "And did so on behalf of the ship which I no longer captain. If you have questions about his recent behaviors, you'd best direct them towards the newest Commander Ceridwen."

He returned to her side, kneeling his penitence. *Better.* "He's already underway on board the *Ceridwen's Cauldron*, your ladyship. This is potentially a galactic security matter. Please." He looked into her eyes, and she allowed his desperate gaze to hold hers. "Will you come with me and answer some questions?"

Galactic security. A long time had passed since she'd been embroiled in anything so dire. Well, she didn't have anything important taking up her time anyway.

"If your needs are so great, we shall accommodate them." She took a deliberate sip from her mug. "After tea."

CHAPTER FOURTEEN

Unorthodox or Illegal?

A week into the trip, Luciano thought he was defending himself well in the pilot house. He'd not caused any further gravity stalls. He'd learned what a space pilot needed to know... so long as everything remained routine.

If something bizarre *did* happen, the pilot on scene would just have to check the *Manual Pilot Manual.* Luciano wouldn't know any better than it would, and he was pretty sure it lived in the pilot house purely to assist with dangerous emergencies.

As usual, he avoided the unpadded pilot chair, intended for a man taller than he. Its supports were in all the wrong places, perfect for digging into muscle and bone. In frustration, he measured the whole two steps across the confined space and pinged Ceridwen's room. She was probably still holed up there.

God forbid she join her Hive or check in on the pilot whom she'd *promised* to relieve as soon as possible.

Her face filled his screen. For all that her hair had frizzed and her skin wore a sheen of sweat, his heart expanded under her gaze until it filled up his chest and pushed his lungs to the side, making it hard to breathe. Her normally piercing gaze seemed unfocused. He had to do something that would make her concentrate on him.

"Hey, Luciano." Her eyes drooped at the sides. "I'm a bit busy right now."

What exactly did she think was more important than keeping her promises to him? Couldn't she read while on piloting duty? She'd sworn that she'd come up and let him teach her the pilot's liturgy, that she'd send him down to Medical as soon as they were safely underway.

Well, her working hours had come, and it was time to tell her that. "Why don't you come up to the pilot house for a lesson today, my lady?" He used the title like a lever, to remind her of her duties.

It didn't work. She sighed a sweet breath that he couldn't smell, trapped as he was in an olfactory cocoon that reflected his own sweat and exhalations. "I really need to get up to speed on all this material about ship owning and cargo runs and explorations. But I'll come by tomorrow, all right?"

Don't worry about tomorrow; tomorrow will be anxious for itself.

He tried to keep the accusation out of his voice when he said, "That's what you told me yesterday."

She dramatically raised one hand into the frame, leaning her head against its fingertips. The pose distorted her countenance into long-suffering contempt. "Look. This stuff is important, okay? And there's a lot of it. I just need some time. If I make it to you tomorrow, that's great. If I don't, I'll get there when I can." She straightened and took her hand back out of the frame, as if she could turn the teasing smile on and the contempt off. "Of course, this'll go faster if no one keeps calling me to interrupt, right?"

She definitely wasn't coming up to learn and relieve him today, then. Didn't she realize that no one knew how to keep an eye on things while he slept?

He grumbled, "Right," and ended the call. He supposed he should've waited for her to do it. She was *Queen*, after all. But if he'd had to look at her for one more moment, his heart would have withered and his lungs would have dried up, and where would that have put the ship? It'd put the *Cauldron* without a pilot, that's where.

Fuck! He slammed a hand against the wall next to the built-in screen, popping open a panel in the process. *Double-fuck!* There were no spare things to throw in the efficient pilot house, no space to pace, no compatriots to yell with.

He re-secured the panel and flashed a message to Alan. *Going to the dining room. Need to rant. Meet me there?* If Alan got the message in time, he'd show up. They had taken to getting lunch together, cementing a new friendship based on mutual love of math and their Queen-

Commander. Luciano and Alan both gave their true Devotion, and that made them strange allies in a sea of unorthodoxy.

Of course, that didn't mean that they understood each other. Luciano had more than once slipped into speaking his native Italian when describing a childhood story. Alan's Alcubierre tensor jet project mystified Luciano whenever Alan showed off a tiny piece of hand-melted plastic or whined things like "Our people should have done this two hundred years ago! Yes, I'm wonderful and a genius, but there's no reason someone else couldn't have started on this. We were the first civilization in space, and we just frittered that away."

He stalked the halls without looking at their functional walls, full of more panels to pop in an aggravated moment. The little ship took bare minutes to traverse entire. In moments, he closed on his destination.

Inside the kitchen, he saw Alan and the politician facing each other, but they had yet to see him. The two were of a height, taller than Luciano though not obnoxiously so, but the politician's flappy-sleeved tunic created a looming effect. Alan did not appear fazed by the illusion of height and breadth. He stood as he usually did, a slightly padded rock which the politician could not intimidate.

Luciano hid behind the dining room door, listening.

"—tell your university." The politician threatened in a nasal, reedy voice that reminded Luciano of his little sister winding down from a tantrum. "No Queen will ever trust you again."

Alan laughed his confident mockery. "Was I ever going to find a great Queen? At my age?" His tone was low and dark. Luciano realized for the first time that Alan's deep voice made him sound like a much older man, something he'd never noticed when they spoke face-to-face.

The politician's answered with a hyena-high bark. In an even more childish voice, he asked, "Oh, so you think your mommy will ride to the rescue?" He made a *tsk* with his tongue and palate. "Just think, you could be at her side forever."

Luciano's shoulders shivered against the wall's cold metal. He'd never asked about Alan's family, not feeling entirely ready to talk about his own. He loved his mother, but wouldn't want to Devote to her. He'd bet Alan felt the same.

The dining room stood silent. Had the pair left through some other exit?

No. Alan spoke again, slow and inexorable. "I'm far too smart to waste. My advisor would never let me to go to a non-physics-related Hive." His pitch wavered on *physics*.

A violent clap came from within the room, sharp contrast to the quiet conversation and secretive threats. Luciano took a deep breath, but couldn't find the air, so he sucked more and more, lost for oxygen.

The politician said. "Your advisor might have second thoughts when he learns you've joined an illegal Hive."

Illegal! Yes, parts of the Hive were suspect, such as having another girl around, especially one who was attached to a Devoted. Still, this couldn't be a criminal Hive. He trusted Rhiannon to keep him. She'd hold him safe and loved and on the path to success.

His respiration sped up, unable to maintain his heart on its regular intake. His lungs knotted.

Could he truly trust Rhiannon? He hadn't seen her in days. She'd abandoned him to the pilot house for a week already, burying his needs and interests underneath her own.

It's a Queen's right to use her Hive as she sees fit.

The reminder didn't help him breathe any better.

Footsteps thundered on the hard floor. The politician delivered one last, ominous line. "Think about it and come to see me if you need help. You can escape this. You don't have to side with these criminals."

Something inside Luciano broke. It wailed betrayal and remorse. The walls of Devotion around it had crumbled, unable to maintain strength without air.

No wonder Rhiannon seemed uninterested in building up his experience or career, didn't talk about getting home again or deferring her college admission. She never intended to finish her education or ascend to her rightful place in society. She was taking improbable chances and pulling a whole Hive down with her.

A Hive he couldn't escape, wouldn't escape, on his honor-bound oath. What a fool he'd been! What forgiveness could he beg so that God would still let him save his sister from a life of mining and underachieving? What sort of life would he lead himself, subsumed to his Queen's capricious desires?

If only the politician would offer his help and friendship to Luciano! But even if he'd never sworn his entire being to Rhiannon, the politician wouldn't be interested in the some know-nothing miner's kid from Dyfed3. Luciano didn't have the family connections to make bribing him worthwhile.

Fuck again.

He almost missed when Alan wandered past his hiding place, head in the clouds and eyes glazed.

"Hey, Alan." Luciano fell in step beside him and bumped shoulders companionably.

The other Hive member jumped and swiveled his head wildly. Alan fled down the corridor, leaving Luciano alone.

Maybe sneaking up on someone who has just been attacked by a blackmailer wasn't the best idea. What else did Llewellyn say that I didn't hear?

God, Luciano needed to talk with someone now more than ever. He headed back to the pilot house to write a letter home that he'd probably never send.

CHAPTER FIFTEEN

Losing Control

Beads of overwarm moisture formed in Rhiannon's hairline as she leaned over her pad. She raked back the frizzes they clung to. How was she supposed to be a good Queen and an effective ship owner if no texts definitively described basic knowledge? A Perceiver could extrapolate from a solid data foundation, yes, but her predictions and decisions would wobble without that initial structure.

Rhiannon threw her pad down on the bed, watching it bounce on her crimson duvet. The dark shock of color bounced and wobbled, lending her barren walls a reflected glory.

Someone scratched at her door. She rocketed to her feet, ready to get away from the helpless quest for a little while. She ignored the headache that came with standing so quickly. *It's just rushing blood*. If she were lucky, Gwyn would wait on the door's other side, wanting to talk again about animals or boys or life outside Rhiannon's self-imposed bedroom-cum-study-carrel.

She unsealed the door, pleased to discover Gwyn. She was less pleased that Victor and Gavin followed behind. Still, she needed a break, and these visitors *were* her friends and Devoted. She ushered them in and sat Gwyn on the bed. The men could stand.

Note to self: Get some more furniture.

Victor slouched against her wall, not meeting anyone's eyes, his face blank and hands shoved into his pockets. In contrast, Gavin stood tall, towering over the rest. But then, everyone looked tall to Rhiannon. She joined Gwyn on the bed and waited for her callers to broach whatever subject brought them.

And waited. And waited.

"Soooo." She drew out the sound. "Why the visit?"

Victor only slouched farther. Gwyn clasped her hands in her lap. Those two clearly weren't talking. Rhiannon arched her eyebrows at Gavin, since he seemed the most composed.

"The passenger, Llewellyn," he said.

Rhiannon expected him to continue, but Gavin stopped there, as if naming the man were answer enough. She drew in a noisy breath, gathering her patience and as much air as possible through her over-heated nose. "Yeeees?" Again she drew out the word, letting the vowels

142

spool out to coax any further thoughts. Her burgeoning headache kept her from tilting her head in curious question, for all that it would surely add to the effect.

"What are you going to do about him?"

As always, Gavin spoke his words like a recital. Had he practiced what to say? Was he quoting one of his mother's plays? His mouth was a flat line across his face, betraying nothing. Sometimes Gavin's off-planet background made him impossible to understand.

Victor kicked against his leaning wall for momentum and launched himself at her, his face a blotchy pink-and-blue. His sleeves twisted all around his arms, but somehow managed not to hamper his movement. "You have to get rid of him!" He caught her shoulders and shook. "I'll help you get rid of him."

Her aching head pounded at the motion.

"He's going to be gone in a few days when we reach the English rendezvous?" she offered.

Victor released her with a little shove that sent her back down to the mattress.

Anger begets violence, but why is he so angry?

Gwyn helped her up with an apologetic smile, but gave no indication of what had so riled the boys.

Gavin snorted. "And when he's gone home and told everyone about our little Hive, how long until someone comes after us? How long until we're jailed for our sins? Will shielding absolution fall from your lips, or will the sin-kiss transmit our doom?"

Rhiannon took a moment to translate that. *No idea what he's quoting. The context would probably help.*

"Are you telling me that Llewellyn knows about Gwyn?" She gestured to her best friend, and saw the menfolk nod. "And that he's threatening us with"—she paused because she hadn't gotten that exactly—"with jail?"

Gavin shook his head. "With our own imaginations," he explained. "He hasn't specifically said *jail* or *hard labor* or *revoked status*. But we all know whatever the Senedd decides won't be good. Our little scheme tips on a fulcrum's point."

Rhiannon needed time to think. She needed space in her aching head and in her cabin so that she could curl up on her duvet and pattern out what Llewellyn might want. How to extricate her people from this shandivang. The room blurred in her overtired eyes. She stood from the bed, all angles and tightly leashed muscles, and pointed at her door. This posture, one text had told her, was a command posture.

"Get out," she ordered them all. "Out."

She'd find a way to fix this. To fix the fox in their midst. The Hive was her responsibility, even if the scheme had been Victor's to start. She wouldn't let them get caught up in *jail* or *hard labor* or *revoked status* or *ANYTHING*.

"No." Gavin's reply came just as calmly and filled with as much harnessed energy as her own. "If you can't solve this puzzle, then you're not a real Queen. You don't care about your Hive." He looked for a moment as though he might vomit, but shook it off and relaxed all his muscles. Releasing the anger. Releasing the fight's urgency. "I really thought you could do this whole Queen thing, you know? I mean, I thought the whole Dyfed Queen system was stupid, but I believed in your ability to make it work."

He turned away from her, away from them all. "I guess you can't."

It was getting hard to breathe. There were too many people. Too many needs. Too many accusing voices, outside and inside her head. She needed to offer something, anything, just to make them all be quiet! *Eisht!*

"We could throw him out an airlock."

The four mulled the idea in silence, tasting its simplicity and horror. Then Gwyn laughed, and Victor offered a weak cough, and Gavin said something like *That'd be dramatic, even for me.*

Even with the laughter and the acknowledgement that no killing could be easy, Rhiannon wasn't absolved of responsibility. She'd never read about anything like this. She didn't know what Llewellyn would really do. She wasn't sure how all of her Hive felt about things.

She needed data. "What about Alan and Luciano?" she asked. "We should see how they feel."

Victor snorted. "They're in hiding, just like you," he accused. He grabbed Gwyn's wrist and motioned to Gavin, pulling his crew away to her door. "We'll figure this out ourselves. We don't need you at all!"

Of course they needed her. She was their *Queen*. Though Victor hadn't gotten around to Devoting yet. She couldn't breathe. She needed oxygen. Air! Why couldn't they give her some more time? She could come up with something.

She just needed time. Time and air and calm. Time and air and calm. Time and air. Air.

A loud wailing began. Rhiannon took a moment to realize it hadn't come from her.

CHAPTER SIXTEEN

Ceridwen Lives

The wail cut through Rhiannon's self-pity like the spring on a mousetrap. It circled through her cabin, echoing off the steel-and-Kevlar and making itself known over and over again.

Galvanized by the realization of *Danger!*, she bounded to her ship-linked station. She'd hunt through the protocols to decipher the siren.

She didn't need to. Large scarlet letters flashed on a white background *OXYGEN LEVELS CRITICAL. PRESSURE WILL REACH FATAL LOWS IN 120s. 119s. 118s.*

She felt body-heat behind her and moved to the side, letting Gavin take his turn at her station. In scant seconds, he found the leak location. Scant seconds that might differentiate life or death. Scant seconds that impressed her with his competence. Scant seconds that rolled away her anxiety over Llewellyn.

She needed to focus on this new problem.

Gavin in the lead, the foursome raced through the halls, trusting Gavin for directions. Trusting Gavin to know how to fix it. Trusting.

They skidded to a stop in a room bristling with polished, silvery tanks. Rhiannon had seen these before, but didn't know how they worked.

Gavin dropped to his knees in front of a forty foot cylinder. He popped the floor panel beneath it, ripping out wires and cursing.

Rhiannon stood beside him, head throbbing with the run and the noise and—*Manawyddan's beard!*—the hypoxia. *All the headaches. All the shortness of breath. All the overheating. They weren't from stress. They were signs of oxygen deprivation. How could I have missed that? Missed that for days.*

Unsure how best to help, she took precious moments to observe her other two crew-companions. Gwyn backed off to just inside the door, staying out of the way. Victor hovered at Gavin's shoulder. His hands fluttered towards the tank, then into his pockets. Only to come out and flutter again. He bit his already puffy and blue-tinged bottom lip and muttered something to himself. Whatever the muttering was, it didn't distract Gavin.

It didn't help him either.

A voice rang out, mixing with the wailing sirens. "What's going on? Somebody! Somebody, please! Call up to the pilot house and tell me what's happening?" The voice paused, as if waiting for an answer. She could hear gasping hyperventilation over the speakers. "Rhiannon? Alan? Are you there? Please? I'm sealed in... I need... Rhiannon?"

She hadn't brought her pad with her when she'd followed Gavin. She couldn't flash Luciano a short, reassuring message. And she didn't have time for more than that. She needed to be here. Needed to help fix this. Needed to make space for Gavin to work. To breathe.

First, get Victor out of his way. Again she assumed the posture: straight lines and tightly leashed strength.

"You." She pointed at Victor with her arm at a perfect ninety degree angle. The command in her voice startled him into obedience. "Read off the warnings." She pointed to another screen that fluctuated with words and graphs. Maybe Gavin already knew everything the screen was saying, but maybe it'd help. Besides, it got Victor doing something positive.

Under her willpower and not his own, Victor moved to the screen. "Red line, main tank at fifteen percent."

To Gwyn, she snapped, "Go change the lithium filters." It couldn't hurt to clean out the air filtration system. Whether or not the problem had anything to do with the carbon-monoxide scrubbers. And it'd give Gwyn something to do.

The remaining air rang with harsh panting over the speakers. "What's going on? My hands look expanded and wrinkled. I'm turning into a puppet! Hello? Rhiannon?

Rhiannon!"

Gavin looked like he needed another pair of non-puppet hands. He had one tool in his teeth and another behind his ear. She held her hand under his mouth until the pliers dropped into it. He grunted his thanks, then tried to explain. "The airflow regulator is wired backwards. Our oxygen's going outside."

She'd never studied this. All she knew was that air going outside meant bad things for the atmosphere-deprived humans inside. "Can you fix it?"

He held out a hand for the pliers she'd taken from his mouth. She slapped them into his palm. All-speed.

Gavin threw himself across the floor to the foot of another forty-foot tank, this one with a red tape ring around the bottom circumference. Someone had scratched *Auxil.* into the red. Still on the ground, Gavin punched the floor plating to open another panel.

Luciano was crying over the speakers now. "*Ave Maria, piena di grazia, il Signore è con te. Tu sei benedetta fra le donne e benedetto è il frutto del tuo seno, Gesú.*"

She couldn't translate it exactly, but knew it was a plea to a power even higher than his Queen. When this was over, she'd find a way to raise him up. She wouldn't fail her Hive. She'd directed Victor, had helped Gavin so far. She could rule them all. She could be the Queen and Commander they needed.

Silence. The sirens stopped their blaring, retreating to their homes.

A hiccup from over the speakers.

Gavin flopped onto his back, pushing the panel next to his head closed. Sweat darkened his white linen shirt. "Yes." He smiled a smile of exhaustion and victory. "I can fix it. Shipwide oxygen concentration will increase by five percent increments until we reach thirty percent or so overall. It'll help us acclimatize." He looked at the tool in her hand, salvaged from his hair. She pushed the first panel closed as she'd seen him do the second. "Thank you."

He meant it. She could tell. In this moment, everything said was the ultimate truth. Disaster averted. Truth revealed.

A disembodied voice, too loud now that it no longer had to compete with the wailing. "Can someone tell me what just happened, please?"

Rhiannon would do more than that. She was done with hiding and researching. It was time to be *Queen*, though she'd rely on Manawyddan's cleverness to figure out how. It was time to lead her people into a better future.

She took Gavin's pad from his relief-slack hands. Her first act: open a ship-wide call.

"Mandatory dinner tonight. I'll explain everything then."

She'd explain to Luciano what had transpired. She'd explain how the future was going to go. She'd explain that now she was ready to be their Queen and Commander.

Her second act: lie down beside Gavin, putting herself on his physical level like the management texts said would make her people more receptive.

"I'd like you to be ship's Handsman," she said. "I trust you to take care of all these physical things."

She'd originally expected that post to be Alan's, knowing that he not only studied physics but was also working on building a miniature Alcubierre tensor jet in his spare time. She was glad she'd held off on offering it until they'd been underway a while. After this performance, she knew Gavin deserved the responsibility and the trust. Where was Alan? He hadn't shown up in days. She'd have to check on him if he skipped another dinner.

Gods. She hadn't been showing up either. How could they count on her?

No wonder Gavin, Victor, and Gwyn wanted to take over.

Well, that was in the past. She'd be Queen and Commander now. If they gave her a chance.

Gavin tilted his head to rest on her shoulder, and she tried not to startle at the contact. The first friendly touch she'd felt since Gwyn had braided her hair.

His large, blue eyes looked up into her face. "I'd be honored," he said.

She imagined she could hear the bond between them singing, like in the films. She had her chance. She'd do right by them. She'd be the best Queen a Hive could have.

CHAPTER SEVENTEEN

Blackmail

Luciano strolled into the dining room one minute late, daring Rhiannon to notice his defiance. He'd always shown up early to classes, to job sites, to parties. Did she know that? Did it matter to her?

His Queen continued her speech, not pausing to reprimand him. Llewellyn sat on her left, a sucking void. "—is now working, but we only have so much. We'll need to restock our oxygen when we dock at the station tomorrow. Until then, Gwyn will be busy constantly monitoring the carbon scrubbers."

She did, however, look pointedly at first him and then the clock on the opposite wall.

She cares! Oh God, she really cares.

His shoulders relaxed. He hadn't even known that they'd been jammed up to his ears until they fell back to normal height.

His face flushed scarlet. The sudden heat of rushing blood reminded him of the earlier airless cold. He drew a few strong breaths just to make sure that he could.

God, the one time I decide to be a little late, everyone else decides to be early. That's the last time I try this trick.

His Hive mates all sat at the drab, grey dining table, listening to their Commander's announcements. A distance existed between Alan and the rest. Even more distance separated the Hive from the sinister outsider.

Rhiannon was resplendent in the haloed lights, fully in control of her meeting. "I'd also like to thank Gavin for making the necessary fixes and discovering the problem. Gavin, please stand up." The day's hero straggled to his feet and made sweeping bows to each side of the table, bending himself in half. "Gavin is our new Handsman. You should all call on him when you have any physical engineering problem. Congratulations, Gavin."

Luciano slid into a seat next to Alan on the Hive-side and jostled his friend for attention. Luciano smiled a greeting, but Alan didn't smile back. Instead, his startled eyes met Luciano's for a moment before falling to the table. Luciano followed his friend's gaze and watched Alan's thumbnails clean each other, as if that were the most important thing here, as if he weren't listening to Rhiannon or noticing Luciano or letting himself be a part of the evening's conversation.

Alan couldn't give up. Alan, with his genius and his funny way of looking at the universe, was the most alive person on the ship. He couldn't give up on himself and his Hive. Luciano wouldn't let him.

Resolve firmed, Luciano gave himself over to his Queen anew. He reined in the devil under his skin, the baser impulses that exhorted him to throw things and lose faith whenever life got hard. Instead, he rededicated and Devoted inside his own head. *My sword and my service, my body and my blood, my agency and my anima.* They belonged to her, always and forever. As he watched her in the bright lights that illuminated her energy and her purpose, he knew there could be no better Queen for him.

I trust you, Rhiannon. I love you. Trust me back.

She didn't look at him, but she didn't need to. He could feel the connection flowing between them, just as described in the films and the books. Generations had documented the feedback loop of Devotion. His Devotion made her a better Queen. His intense love made her love him back.

If he ever lost her, that feedback would drag him down into an unbalanced depression. That dark spiral could turn good Devoted feral.

Her voice carried throughout the room, ringing truth and power against the walls. Her presence coiled around him, wrapping him in her charisma.

"Going forward, we'll have choices. I've narrowed these down to the most interesting. Going forward, we'll lean on each other to make the right decisions for our

Hive as a whole, not for ourselves individually." She took a moment to single each of them out with her eyes, meeting gazes until Hive members faltered before her, ashamed to ever have acted independently. "Going forward—"

The politician cleared his throat and stood to overlook the room from Rhiannon's side. His height made him seem as though he overlooked her as well. "Going forward," he said, "you'll do me a little favor." His strident nasality, too loud, obliterated the echoes of Rhiannon's speech.

Walk with the Devil! Luciano balled his hands into fists, and saw Alan's head fly up to stare straight at the man. Did the bastard really mean to tread over his Queen? Well, this Hive would teach him a lesson in manners. Luciano looked behind him to the three others. They didn't notice him, too busy gripping each other's hands as though they could save themselves from falling if they just held on to something else.

If he'd have no help from that quarter, then his Queen would stand up for herself, and she'd be pleased to have him stand with her. He sent all his thoughts and anger and muscle into that Devoted feedback loop. He'd lend her the strength to push back, though she'd be fine on her own.

"No, we will not," Rhiannon denied the politician. Luciano rejoiced. She stood for all that was good and sacred in this world, and he loved her intensely for it. "If nothing else, I need to discuss your proposal with my people. Say your piece, sir, and we'll let you know what we decide."

The man flapped his silly sleeves like a stupid owl, *stealing her breath.* "Then I have no choice. You'll do me this little favor, and I won't tell anyone about your illegal activities. This is a matter of life and death, my life and death, and I can't chance your deciding the wrong way."

Luciano shook his head against the term *illegal,* the mere suggestion that their Hive could be so. *Shut your beak, owl.* Rhiannon would set him right. She'd defend their unorthodox structure. She'd explain that the man had no power over him. Luciano noticed for the first time that the passenger and Gwyn were both in the room at once.

Why is she *here?*

Rhiannon bit her lip and pushed her hair behind her ear, looking past everyone and not challenging the passenger's authority.

The man's oil-smoke voice crept in through ears and noses, slimy and unchecked by any barriers of hope. "Don't look so glum, children! It's just a little favor. You'll take this package to coordinates that I give you." He plucked a trunk from the seat beside his former one. "Don't open it, now. It will never do if someone... official should decide to question you about your involvement." A muscle ticked on the side of his mouth, giving him a cruel and uncontrolled look. "Really, that's all. I'll even top up your tanks for you at the station, free of charge. There are perks to saving me from certain demise, as if that good deed weren't a cause worthy enough."

And when they'd completed the deal, for contraband or drugs or some other terrible exchange, how would they pay for fuel and air to return? Would the politician's largesse extend past his delivery date?

The politician gave Rhiannon an overfamiliar kiss on the cheek. The act obscured her from the room, as if he'd eaten her up and hid the evidence in his flappy sleeves. "I'm so pleased to have met you." He took Rhiannon's wrist and rested her hand on top of the delivery trunk. That done, he walked past them all and left the room.

Freed at last from some magical gravity, Luciano rocketed to his feet, pleased to see that Gavin and Victor did as well. *How dare he lay hands on her? Presume to dictate her movement!* They three converged on their stricken Queen, statue-still with her DNA leaking all over the evidence box.

Luciano fell to his knees at her side. He took her hand off the box and laced her frozen fingers through his own. He rested his head against her upper thigh, lending her his heat and his strength. For long moments, he waited for her to regain herself.

He was not disappointed. She squeezed his hand, then dropped it to point at the box. Energy and command emanated from the straight line of her shoulder to her square nail.

"We're going to open this package," she said. "The moment he leaves the *Cauldron*." She lowered her arm, energy sapped once again. "But I'm afraid we'll have to deliver it, no matter what's in there."

She'd confirmed it, then. The politician's story contained a pit of truth. But it didn't matter. Luciano loved her, respected Alan and Gavin, and knew he'd settle into his place here. Even if that place stretched the bounds of legality.

CHAPTER EIGHTEEN

Upload, Download, Reload

Two days after Llewellyn's display of power, the *Cauldron* approached the English station. Luciano hoped to make a better showing of today's docking than he had on departure. He had two weeks of experience now, after all. He envisioned coupling smoothly, dropping off his passenger, and decoupling just as fast.

Soon we'll be rid of the interloper.

Luciano drew a deep breath, not even noticing the sweat-slick aftertaste. Long shifts in the pilot house had inured him to its idiosyncratic ventilation. He knew all the procedures. He could find all the buttons. Just in case, though, he kept the *Manual Pilot Manual* open to the relevant page and readably close—on the floor at his side.

With a shaking hand, he flipped the toggle next to the unlit amber bulb. If he didn't hail the station before they called him, he'd cause a diplomatic incident. "Victoria Station, Victoria Station. This is the Dyfed diplomatic courier *Ceridwen's Cauldron* on approach vector. Do you read me?"

So far, everything seemed in order. The amber bulb hadn't indicated an incoming hail, which meant he'd preceded the station's proximity warnings.

The frequency opened on the station-side. Luciano heard a brief curse before an efficient female voice responded. *"Hail the diplomatic courier,* Ceridwen's Cauldron. *Please come to a complete stop fifty klicks from the green painted hull section. We'll reel you in."*

Even at the slow speed he'd achieved this morning, he was coming up on fifty klicks right fast. He also couldn't see the green section, so Luciano swung the ship—now approved to be in English space—in a wide arc. That provided more time to reduce velocity and to hunt out the specified location.

Victoria Station didn't look any different from Dyfed's spaceport, as far as Luciano could tell. It floated above a Sol-3 type planet and was faced in a dull metal that probably contained Kevlar layers, like a protective sandwich. It was spiked like an old-fashioned sea mine. Those spikes could extend quickly to attach a ship and reel her in.

Luciano couldn't see anything through the station's windows but bright lights, sharp spots of relief against space black and metallic grey. It was larger than the spaceport they'd left, perhaps a bit more rigid. Otherwise, it looked much the same.

Why would it be different? Dyfed spaceport is older, but only by a hundred years. Somehow, though, he'd expected it to be more *English* or at least more modern.

Aha! He spotted the green and angled towards it, then fired a reverse burst. If Llewellyn planned to top up their fuel, then Luciano had no qualms about using the stuff. And, *there!* He came to a floating rest exactly 51.34 klicks from the station. Surely Victoria didn't expect more precision than that.

They didn't. Unfurling like a butterfly's tongue, the docking tentacles slithered towards him. He tried not to feel like a fly about to be caught in a spider's web. The station would let them go. The English didn't even want them around.

Too close to see now, the tether's maws disappeared from his windows. The *Cauldron* shivered and reverberated once, twice. Luciano heard a screech of metal pulling taut, a *thunk* of connection.

The *Cauldron* lurched under the station's power. Victoria reeled her in slowly on five rails. *"Diplomatic courier* Ceridwen's Cauldron, *you are secured for docking. Please turn off all engines or other motion devices. Will you be taking advantage of our fine facilities or baking your carbon filters during your visit?"*

The station loomed closer. Luciano could see the little flags painted onto the green customs section. The one for Dyfed barely took up a billboard's worth. He wouldn't have noticed it if he hadn't been hunting for the red-on-gold Welsh dragon.

"Victoria Station, we have one diplomatic passenger who will be disembarking, and we'll be topping up our supply tanks." Was that enough information?

"Ceridwen's Cauldron, *we'll inform Customs of your intentions. Is there anything else we can help you with today?*"

He couldn't think of anything. No, wait.

"Victoria Station, I have some letters to send back to Dyfed. Do you send mail to Welsh space?"

A long pause tasted like weak tea, bitterly disappointing and overhyped. Finally, the woman returned. "Ceridwen's Cauldron, *station protocol states that you can't access our communications systems from dock. It also suggests that Dyfed ships are expected to make available their... Queens for such duties. Will your Queen be the diplomatic passenger?*"

He didn't trust Llewellyn to send his letters to Mama and Aurelia. He doubted Gavin's mother, Alan's academic advisor, or Rhiannon's father wanted their messages in the politician's grasping hands either.

"Victoria Station, thank you for your suggestions. We'll figure something out."

The efficient voice returned immediately, making up for the earlier delay. "Ceridwen's Cauldron, *understood. You'll deal with Customs and on-station personnel until you leave. When you're ready to depart, send us your flight plan within local space, a copy of your Customs forms, and a passenger manifest. Enjoy your stay. Victoria Station out.*"

How should he tell his Hive mates—his *Queen*—that

they remained cut off from all they knew and loved? The disappointment gobbled up his docking's success. The glow of finding the right buttons and making the perfect stop dimmed.

He put that news off for a few more moments, turning off the requested systems and puttering about in the pilot house. As soon as the *Cauldron* and the station were firmly attached to one another, he'd find Rhiannon. She'd fix everything.

Reminded of his place and his Queen, he smiled broadly at the tentacled station roping them in. The pilot's reflection showed his whole top row of teeth. But that white slice went dark when Customs flashed him their forms. All the questions were about the evil owl's plans and baggage.

Well, that put a stick between the wheels. Much as he didn't want to, he'd have to contact Llewellyn. At least he didn't have to do it in person. Luciano stood and stretched—no reason to stay in the chair's vise—and walked over to the call screen. His luck stayed dismal: the politician answered.

"Why do you interrupt me, young man?" The villain's hair flew in wispy whorls about his head. "I'm busy packing."

"I'm sorry if this is a bad time." Luciano wasn't sorry at all. "Victoria Station has some forms for you." He sent the forms to the politician's shipboard address.

On screen, the blackmailer's pad beeped the forms' receipt. The man looked smaller when doing normal things, like packing and reading on his pad. He wasn't nearly as imposing as he'd seemed on the Night of the Box. He tapped a few things and pressed a thumb to the printbox. "I have this in hand."

Luciano took that for dismissal and reached to shut off the call.

The traitorous bastard interrupted his action. "I see they also request an outgoing passenger manifest. You'll make sure my name is on it when you leave to rendezvous with *Llyr's Llambo*."

Though Llewellyn spoke without niceties—*no hair on this man's tongue*—Luciano didn't believe the blackmailer spoke plainly. "When should we expect you back?"

The man turned away from the camera and shoved more possessions into his off-screen valise. "I won't *be* back." The *you imbecile* was implied. "Let's just say I'm taking a little vacation, but want my bosses to think I'm still on the clock."

That sounded reasonable enough, aside from the part where he wanted Luciano to lie to the English government. Still, the idea tasted like a two-hour pasta sauce: incomplete. "We can wait for you. We're not in a rush." Luciano didn't like structuring his life around the man, but the suggestion had his desired effect.

Explosive, the blackmailer whirled around and got so close to the screen that their eyes didn't line up and the right half of Llewellyn's face didn't fit. "No! No one is in any hurry. But my superiors will want to see proof of a mission carried out." His snarl quelled any further argument.

165

Luciano wanted to ask, *If no one's in a hurry, why not wait?* But Llewellyn still had control of the conversation.

The blackmailer paced. His breathing turned erratic, picked up by the sensitive microphones to travel through the ship and reverberate off the pilot house walls. He waved unimpressive fists and muttered phrases Luciano only caught snatches of: "No reason to send—" and "Time will take care of those de—" and "Try to pull the wool over on *me*, will—"

Llewellyn stopped pacing and smoothed his hands over his wrinkled tunic. Once he'd returned to his initial position in front of the call screen, he said, "You have your orders. That is all." He cut the connection.

Yes, Luciano felt sure that the passenger's request held some deeper meaning than *Civil Servant's Holiday*.

***

It only took a few hours to get Llewellyn off the ship and the provisions topped up. Of course, Llewellyn had been part of making air, fuel, and food arrive so quickly.

Station delivery had informed them, "Well, you're not full up, but that's all you paid for. Don't go leaving your gates wide open and hopeful, now. You'll leak all that good oh-two and propellant right back to us, and you can't get any more."

Which left Luciano with even more bad news to impart. He hadn't sent their letters home, and they might not have enough supply to get back from wherever their evil duke intended to send them.

"Oh, *Gesú*." He breathed realization like a prayer, a prayer that he might be wrong. The technician had said the ship couldn't stay plugged into the station as far as air and fuel were concerned, and Luciano knew he'd never disconnected at Dyfed spaceport.

"Oh, *Gesú*," he said again. "The air leak was my fault." The realization was bitter as chicory.

His legs turned to ice. He checked his hands, making sure they hadn't puffed or wrinkled with hypoxia. His breath sped up, like it had that day. "My fault."

CHAPTER NINETEEN

Knock Yourself Out

The day after they left Victoria Station behind, Victor met with Gavin for their daily quarterstaff practice. Gavin had lent him a retractable metal staff, and Victor had been practicing on his own until his muscles rebelled. Until this impossible situation melted away. Until Llewellyn's blackmail and Gwyn's nervous standoffishness didn't matter.

When he concentrated on the movements, his mind quieted. He didn't have to worry about finding his purpose on the ship. About leaving home. He could just be.

Gavin extended his own staff, the metal opening up like a lethal flower in the springtime sun. "Drills first," he said.

Side by side, they moved through the drills. Upper right block, upper left block, lower right block, lower left block, overhead block, squat for the knee block. Repeat fifty times. Repeat with strikes instead of blocks for another fifty.

Victor made his thirtieth practice block. "So, what do you think the stuff in the box is really for?"

They'd opened the box as soon as Llewellyn left. Plastic squares they could confirm as money and bags of a white powder that they didn't know how to analyze.

Gavin wasn't even breathing hard. "Ah, drugs and money. The scourge of youth across the universe." His unrecognizable quotations were a lot less annoying when you were already practicing to beat him up.

"Right." Victor grunted as he switched his practice mode to *attack*. It required more force. "But why? Who needs drugs *and* money? Don't you usually use one to get the other?" They were in perfect synch, side by side on bare metal floors.

We ought to pick up some mats for the gym area at our next destination. If we survive to see it.

Separate warm-ups complete, they faced each other. Bowed formally.

Gavin suggested, "How about a crime ring? They'd take their skim off the top of every game in town." He used a strange American accent for the bit starting at *skim*. He attacked, and Victor blocked on the upper right, upper left. Practice, practice, practice.

"That little? It'd never happen. Llewellyn's part of something dangerous, but it's not that sort of organized crime. It's costing him just as much to send us out there as it would to sell that stuff."

Gavin just shrugged, which didn't throw off his next attack to Victor's head. "We'll learn more when we get there. Speaking of getting places, have you heard about Alan's ludicrous project?"

No, because Alan doesn't talk to me. You two are bonding over some mutual respect-hatred, and I don't belong at all.

"Aren't you even a little curious about the creeps we're meeting?" Victor's turn came to attack. He brought down his staff to the upper right with as much force as he could muster.

Gavin stumbled back. "He's got this miniaturized tensor jet. I saw some of the force-to-distance projections yesterday. But that Hawking radiation's going to be a killer." He giggled at his own joke. Hawking radiation could cook a ship inside its bubble. It was always a killer.

Victor didn't laugh with him. Alan and his stupid project didn't have a place in this gym. Still. "How miniature are we talking?"

Gavin resumed his attacks now, adding in some odd side-body ones that Victor hadn't seen before. "Well, it fits on the ship."

Victor snorted. That didn't tell him much. "In his room?" Block, block, block.

Gavin circled him, crouching low to the ground like a wolf or a martial arts actor. "I haven't seen it. Haven't seen much of Gwyn lately either."

What is this? Must we talk about every frustrating subject in my life during my favorite downtime? He shivered in his sweat, but didn't shake his head to clear salt from

170

the area around his eyes. He'd be on alert when Gavin pounced.

"She says everything's fine." *But I don't believe her.* It was time for a subject change. "Luciano's on kitchen duty tonight."

Gavin finally sprang, telegraphing every move as he raised his staff overhead. Victor could have tried to ram his own weapon into his friend's solar plexus, but the point of practice was to *practice*. Not to improvise. Dutifully, he raised his staff overhead with both hands, letting the blow hit dead center and slide off. Successfully blocked.

"Thank the gods," said Gavin. "I swear, in faith 'tis passing strange, 'tis passing strange the taste of the food he makes. But at least he can cook."

I know that one! "Are you misquoting *Othello* at me?"

Gavin laughed and struck out a blow to his left shoulder. "You're learning!" he crowed, just as the staff met its mark with a sharp thud.

Victor fell back, crumpling to the floor to cradle his shoulder. It was just a shock, not true pain. The unyielding floor against his knees, however... "That fucking hurt." Heat spread out from the meaty muscle, making his whole upper body tingle with the impact. He rotated the bone in the socket. Nothing twinged.

Gavin held out a hand to help him up. "Let's go find Gwyn and misquote some more."

Well, it wasn't a good idea, but it was an idea. "After we scour shower all this sweat off."

Gavin nudged him in the good shoulder. "Have to smell attractive for the ladies, eh?"

Victor shrugged. The action made his left arm heat up again, and he bit his lip to distract from the sensation. "You're not curious about the delivery *at all*?"

CHAPTER TWENTY

Delivery Day

This was the most crowded Rhiannon's command center had ever been. While the pilot still sat up in the pilot house, the remainder of her Hive stood with her beneath it. They made an oasis of humanity, surrounded by blinking consoles full of possibilities that defied her current understanding.

No windows showed the reality outside. She could only guess.

After Llewellyn's departure, they'd opened the box to find a few baggies of some unknown substance atop a bed of plastic deposit squares. Rhiannon hadn't known whether to be dismayed or unsurprised.

Now, a week from the start of this whole blackmail scheme, her *Cauldron* floated in space across from another ship. The *Llyr's Llambo* was a third again larger than the *Cauldron* and darker, a black blot on the emptiness of space. What kind of people trafficked drugs and money out here? What kind of people lived in that gloomy vessel?

No matter. She'd make the delivery. Then her Hive could get out of the situation and the area. Could get back on a legitimate path. Could get outsystem and be free. Maybe they could apprentice themselves to a larger, more experienced ship until they were ready to strike out on their own. *Luciano in particular will like that, finally getting Medical training.*

Speaking of Luciano... She wrapped sweaty palms around the ladder rungs and ascended to the pilot house. She peeked her head over the floor and asked, "Are our friends still out there?"

He jumped and bashed his head against his chair's headrest. *Oops.*

"Hey," he said. Sometimes she wondered what Luciano was thinking about. A simple *Hey* didn't give her much to go on. "Yeah. They're hovering. They haven't tried to contact us, though, I don't think."

She nodded to acknowledge his report and firmed her mouth. The texts said that would make her look serious. "Right. Let's fix that." She dropped back down to the command room's floor where the rest of her Hive waited. They should be present for this momentous communication. They shouldn't have to wait for her second-hand story about the vile criminals who held their lives in taloned hands.

At her motion, Alan placed a ship-to-ship call, audio only. They waited. They waited for the talks to begin. They waited for this madness to end. They waited for danger or absolution.

"Hello?" It was a man's voice. Gravelly and hopeful. "Who's there?"

Her turn. "This is Commander Ceridwen of *Ceridwen's Cauldron*. I've, uh, got your package. How do you want it delivered?"

"It? It!" The man was not happy about how she'd described his box of drugs and money. "By all means, tell me your plans for delivering *it*."

Uh, okay. "Do you have anything for making a deep space transfer?" Because she certainly didn't. Or, if she did, she didn't know what it was or where it lived. *Life would be so much easier with magical teleporters. I'll have to get Alan on inventing that.* She quashed an inappropriate giggle at the thought of Alan casting spells over his equipment and chanting bizarre physics formulae whenever they needed to send an object or person across long distances.

The man harrumphed, the sound like rocks sliding against each other before settling in a precarious pile. "We'll attach our boarding tube. You can come over and bring *it* with you, your ladyship." His use of her title was anything but obsequious.

The call went silent.

"He cut the transmission," Gavin said unnecessarily. Incredulously. "I thought your people didn't hang up on Queens. That it was a point of honor."

Rhiannon shrugged. Who knew with criminals, after all? "Our people, Gavin? We're your people too."

He just smiled at her. "As you say, my lady." She could tell he didn't mean it. Ah well. He still followed her lead. That was the important part. Plus he was charming in his own, over-the-top, thespian manner.

On the floor at her left, mostly out of the way, the forbidden merchandise seemed almost apologetic. It hid in her shadow, not calling attention to itself. Well, no more. She hoisted it in her arms, forcing it into the spotlight.

"I'll just head over and drop this off then," she said.

"No!" Alan shouted, then patted at his voice box as if surprised by the outburst. His hands hovered around his head. His mouth opened in a wavering oval. "You can't go by yourself. I'll come with you." She wanted to argue, but he cut her off. "It's my right to be at your side." His eyebrows flew high above wateringly wide eyes.

She could only acquiesce as gracefully as possible, with a genteel dip of the head. She didn't want to lead anyone into potential danger, but he did have the right to demand access to her presence. As her Devoted, his place could always be with her. To deny that truth would be to deny his Devotion.

Victor said, "You should take Gavin too, for protection."

How odd. Gavin just made Handsman, not Security.

"Nothing against Gavin, but why would my Handsman want to come with me?"

Victor leaned a hip against a console on the room's outskirts and slouched. He looked down at his hands and cracked his knuckles as he pursued the topic. "Gavin's been teaching me to use a quarterstaff. He's good with stage combat. If you get in trouble..."

He didn't need to finish that sentence. It hung in the air like a match ready to strike.

Sound reasoning. She could order Gavin's attendance on her, but she'd prefer he volunteer, especially since he still referred to Devotion as something that originated outside of his own culture.

"Gavin?"

His permanent semi-smile faded as he frowned, not at her nor Victor, but at Alan who had settled into place at her right. *They're still fighting from that first meeting? Brigid's tits! That's some grudge.* She hadn't realized their early animosity still lingered. She'd have to work on that.

"Yeah," he said. "I'll go. My sword and my anima and all that."

Only when he was discussing Devotion did Gavin's voice lose its grandiloquence. Only then did he sound like a surly teenager who sat in the back row and drew infinity symbols on the desks.

"Great!" she said, injecting happiness into her voice and hoping to make them all optimistic by vibrating *positivity molecules* about the cabin. "Let's get suited up and head out."

***

177

The suits for spacewalking didn't look like much. A thin coating of paint crackling over a centimeter-thick rubbery skin that tapered to the barest membrane around the hands. Was the paint the important part? In which case, the cracks were troubling. Or was the skin the important part? In which case, what was it?

This Rhiannon hadn't studied yet. She had to hope and trust that the suits were in working order. That she could put one on correctly. They looked like unflattering jump suits with hoods, but she had no intention of missing some complicated necessity purely because it was anathema to planetary fashion.

She plucked a red-coated one from a locker, glad that her favorite color came in her approximate size. She watched Alan grab a blue one, and Gavin a utilitarian black which might have been coated or might have been just the rubbery stuff. She dawdled as though checking the lines of her suit and studied Gavin from the corner of her eye. He donned his suit like footie pajamas, right over his regular clothes—regular for flamboyant Gavin anyway.

She copied him. *Please, clever Manawyddan, don't let me fall over or put this on wrong or miss a fastener that'll mean embarrassment or death.* She secured her hood with its flimsy, plasticky window to the front. With her hands already in gloves, at least she didn't have to worry about getting fingerprints on the faceplate.

"Ready?" she asked her escort.

They didn't reply. Not that she could hear, at least.

There was probably a communications device in these things. Probably. Well, they'd just have to do without since there was no time for experiments. She reached up and grabbed their shoulders, propelling them towards the airlock door and letting go. Her gloves rasped against her hands, pulling at the whorls in her skin before going sweat-slick inside the rubber.

Guess I won't have to worry about hangnails.

She waved a hand at the camera in the ceiling, just in case the rest of her Hive was watching.

Time to test these suits. She gestured to the airlock door.

Alan tapped something on the console next to the door before picking up the delivery box. Gavin leaned against the spoked wheel on the portal's face. She imagined it creaking with disuse.

I'm sure the last crew used this thing all the time. It'll be fine. She wiggled toes that were starting to feel damp in their socks.

The door opened, the ship's air rushing past and into the new zone. She breathed the air inside her hood. In, out, in out, in.

So far, still alive.

They repeated the process on the next door, this one to the wild macrocosm. No air *whoosh*ed this time. Beyond the door, a beige accordion tube connected her ship and the other. She placed her foot on the first ridge and wobbled there. Without a solid floor, she'd be certain to lose her balance at least once. If she fell, she'd have to place even more trust in her crumbling red container.

179

She tightened her abdominal and gluteal muscles and stood as straight as possible. *Balance comes from the core*, her mother used to admonish when they danced around the gardens. *Let your stomach hold you up, not your feet or your ankles.* She advanced, leading her companions like a Queen-Commander should.

Quarterway down the tunnel. If nothing else, her mother's advice was giving her a workout. She hadn't fallen yet. She checked over her shoulder to make sure her Devoted were still there. *Good.*

Halfway down the tunnel. Her foot didn't make contact with the accordion bridge's next ridge. She gasped, tasting stale air and sweat with the back of her throat. But she didn't fall. Didn't hit the tunnel's floor and rupture her death-defying protective shell.

She just floated there, waiting, her body unable to progress with nothing to fight against. *Weightlessness.* This far from each ship, neither artificial gravity held any power. A black form rushed past her, arms extended, and she went blind.

Well, not blind exactly. She blinked her eyes and shook her head to get the frizzy brown hair out of her vision. Some of it refused to move, sweat-stuck to her forehead. The rest flitted about, but enough dislodged that she could make out her path again. She emulated Gavin's swimming arms.

Three-quarters of the way down the tunnel. Now she understood why Gavin hadn't gone fully horizontal. Here the gravity made a sudden comeback. Only her upright carriage and still-ready muscles saved her from stumbling when she landed.

Ship achieved. As on the *Cauldron*, this one had both permission-based and manual locking systems. As they would have on their own ship, Alan made the computerized request and Gavin turned the wheel-handle.

Then they were on their own in hostile territory.

Inside, the other ship's airlock looked like their own. Small, bare, airless. Once they'd sealed the room back up, Gavin pounded the side of his fist on *Llyr's Llambo*'s inner door. It didn't make any sound, at least none that she could hear in her moist, sense-muffling helmet. But it must have alerted the people on the other side, meaning the lock had the necessary atmosphere, because the door opened.

Through the hair stinging her eyes, she saw a staging room much like their own. It held grey metal lockers, presumably full of suits, and uncovered floors. Directly in the doorway stood a middle-aged gentleman—maybe sixty years old?—with reddish-brown hair and crow's feet next to his eyes. He looked nice enough for a drug dealer.

Gavin preceded her onto the ship, then Alan. They both moved out of the way, off to the sides and out of her sightline. She stepped onto the deck and waited while the ship's crew closed their airlock door.

The gentleman gestured that she could take off her helmet.

I'd love to take off the rest of the suit too. Then I could empty all this sweat out of my boots! She was careful with the fastenings, no matter how much she craved the fresher, cooler air.

Free at last, she raked a hand through her scraggly hair. Then she stopped, fingers barely past her ear-line. Next to the almost nice-looking man, a white-haired gent waved a knife at a terrified Alan. On her other side, two other men covered Gavin.

Well, they had a right to be worried, she supposed. Who knew what dealings between criminals looked like?

The box rested at Alan's feet. She moved slowly, trying not to provoke any reaction as she hefted it. Heart beating hard enough to make the thick spacesuit she wore shudder, she slowed her breathing. It was one text's trick to making herself appear calm and in control.

"I believe this is what you wanted." She offered the box to the man in front of her.

He growled—actually growled!—and swatted the box from her hands. It smashed against the lockers, the loud crash echoing. Everyone winced. "What in Annwyn's bloody Otherworld is that supposed to be? Where is she?" The man reduced his voice to a gravelly whisper that she recognized from the audio-only. "Where is *it*?"

Ummm. *If this isn't what he wants, then what is?* She didn't have time to ask.

The white-haired gent dropped the knife to fly at her, delivering a solid punch to her jaw. All low-tech fighting so as not to damage the ship in battle. She fell hard against the floor, pain and bruises blossoming inside her hip. Down to the bone. She raised her hand to her face. No blood.

She opened her mouth to say *something,* and a scream pierced the air. Anguished and primal and not her own. Alan, scientific Alan, leapt onto her attacker. He scratched and bit and pulled. All the while wailing his pain and horror.

A boot knocked against her head. Headache and ringing filled her skull until they reached a fever pitch. Until she heard nothing. Saw nothing.

Felt nothing at all.

CHAPTER TWENTY-ONE

The Road to Freedom

Luciano had never been inside a jail cell before. All that propaganda about the miners of Nuova sleeping off a drunk at the local Motel Polizia was just wishful thinking from the Cymric superiorists on Dyfed.

It had the expected amenities: cots, toilet and wash-basin, electrified metal bars on the doors. Little lived-in touches, though, surprised him. For instance, intricately patterned rugs covered the outside hallway with red and cream, and a trio of blown glass vases sat in an artful arrangement on the end table next to his cot.

Who put that sort of thing in a jail cell? Clearly the *Llyr's Llambo* didn't see much criminal action.

At least he wasn't alone. Not only had the mobster thugs demanded all *Cauldron* personnel come aboard their ship, but he shared this box with Alan. Rhiannon had a matching cell across the way. Luciano could see a lush, velvety blanket keeping his unconscious Commander warm. When he'd made his displeasure known to their captors—screamed, really—about being separated from his Queen, they'd made pointed remarks about letting him see her, about how they weren't heartless monsters who separated Devoted from devotee.

He worried where his other three Hive mates were being held, but this was enough for him. If he and Alan and Rhiannon could escape, they could find a way to get the others out later. His friend and his Queen were the most important. If their jailers were to be believed, the others must not have been distraught about leaving Rhiannon behind. Otherwise, they too would have ring-side seats to whatever horrid tortures the criminals might think up for his Queen.

Mother Mary, don't let them hurt her.

The thought spurred him like an axe in the back. He launched from his cot to pace the cell's meticulously staggered hardwood floorboards. The cot shuddered from the weight loss as he rose. It skittered to the side with a shrieking clatter that made Alan start.

A glance across the way proved Rhiannon was still too out of it to notice.

Alan settled back onto his cot. His sightless eyes turned to the wall behind the vases. *God, that's creepy.* The animated maybe-genius was like a dead bishop finding himself at the gates of Hell, confused about how he'd ended up there and unable to fathom his change in status.

Luciano didn't know what exactly was bothering his friend, but he wasn't going to waste Alan's talents. There'd be no coddling here.

"Get up, man. We've got work to do."

At least his voice knocked Alan from his self-involved stupor. Alan turned towards him and shook his head. "Me? Work?" He laughed like a brook of contaminated water. "What good is my work? Where was I during the oxygen debacle? What does it matter?" Finished with this self-defeatist invective, he returned to his mopey slump. "What do I matter?"

This melancholy ran deeper than a fear of imprisonment. Alan's issues had festered longer than a mere few hours of jail time. Well, whatever Alan's personal problems or desires to be left alone, Luciano needed his skills. Of the two of them, only one had a chance of breaking out of this joint... and it wasn't the guy whose name began with the letter *L*.

Channeling an uncle from the *tough love* school of life, he dragged Alan from the cot. He shoved his cellmate's face next to the bars, staying shy of their dangerous touch, and shook him.

I'm sorry, Alan.

"Look at that," he demanded. Alan's eyes remained resolutely closed, his resignation total. Luciano wouldn't have it. "Look at your Queen. There she lies, helpless and hopeless. Will you leave her to the carrion crows? Or will you rise to her rescue?"

The muscles under his hand went rigid. They filled with blood and vigor and a taut dislike, though of Luciano or himself or the criminals, only Alan knew. Luciano didn't ask as Alan inspected the door. He had no plans to interrupt this spurt of agency.

He'd have to keep Alan frothing over Rhiannon and her possible doom. They didn't have time to worry about their own problems or desires. Now was the time to act, to escape!

Alan finished his inspection and headed back to the cots. *Damn it. Not again.* Luciano steeled himself to screw his friend's fears a little tighter.

He didn't need to.

With a great heave and a crash, Alan splintered one of the green vases into tinkling shards. The young man rummaged through the remains, slicing open a finger that poured slick vermillion onto the sparkling glass, until he chose a favorite piece. He returned to the door.

Alan pried at a seam in the wall next to the bars with his glass lever, humming the tenor line to "Men of Harlech" as he pushed and cajoled the metal. Before he mumbled out *Freedom's cause is the strongest* for the fifth time, a section of wall screeched free. The metal bonged against Alan's head on its way down to scratch the warm, brown flooring.

The welded wall no longer united, he tore at the hole.

"Help me with this," he ordered Luciano. Together, they pulled and strained until it widened to show a mess of color-coded wiring. Luciano stopped when the engineer did and waited for instructions.

They didn't appear to be forthcoming. Alan stared at the exposed worms and junction boxes, eyes traversing paths that Luciano couldn't follow.

Alan went back to his pile of debris and selected a smaller glass shard. He sawed at a blue-coated wire with it, still mumble-humming "Men of Harlech," while Luciano hovered over his shoulder.

Freedom thickest walls can batter / Fate is in her breath.

A red-coated wire was next. Alan twisted the blue and red together in some unfathomable way before plucking a box from its insulated nest.

"So, ah, what are you doing?" Luciano didn't want to be a useless lump who asked too many stupid questions and got in the professional's way. He didn't. He just wanted to help, and maybe to understand what was going on.

Alan was hummumbling away, *"Thickest walls can batter,"* but interrupted his song to answer. "I'm getting down to a place where I can trigger the emergency protocols. You know, all that *in event of fire* stuff." He put his flaking, blood-crusted tool in his teeth in order to do something with the wall's innards, something Luciano couldn't even see.

"That sounds like something you'd see in a film. Can anyone do that?"

Alan pulled his grease-covered hands out of the wall and turned to give Luciano his full, incredulous attention. Sarcasm dripped from his voice when he cheerily said, "Why, yes. Anyone can do it, just like anyone can work on my miniature tensor jet project. It's a wonder we have jail cells at all when the prisoners are all on the honor system."

The joyful disdain made an eerie combination.

Luciano sucked his lips under his teeth and looked down. The slide of flesh over enamel shocked him out of growing embarrassment and he grinned ruefully. "So you're saying it's a complicated surgery then."

Alan's eyebrows flew up at the analogy. He cocked his head and shrugged. "I'd have said magic, but sure. It's a complicated surgery. Call me the only hardware doctor on staff who can bring this patient back to life." He turned back to the jumbled intestines and made a few more passes with his magic hands.

"This last bit is delicate," he whispered more to himself than to his audience. "And..."

Alan's voice trailed off as he searched the hallway from rug to light fixture. With a whoop, he pulled Luciano into the one-armed hug common to affectionate men on Dyfed. Luciano still hadn't gotten the hang of those Dyfed-style hugs, though. He completed the affectionate action with the rest of his body, like any good Italian man would. For a brief moment, he felt his friend's muscle and fat from chest to belly. Then the moment was over. Alan didn't appear to have even noticed the increased contact, too caught up in his apparent success.

The lack of judgment warmed Luciano. "Congratulations," he said, even though he had no idea what had so pleased his Hive mate. "What do we do now?"

"Now we try the door," said Alan. "I didn't trip the shipwide fire alarm, but that could also mean that I didn't trip our emergency fire procedures." He made a shooing motion. "Well? Go on then. Use those strong, hearty muscles."

With a grin, Luciano heaved on the bars, flinching away from the electric shock that never came. He pulled at the door with straining deltoids that heated under his shirt. He'd feel the burn later. He pushed, wedged, and slid. All to no avail.

"Hold on," Alan said. He did something else with the wall's dry intestines. "Try it again."

Once more, Luciano tore the door inward with all his might. This time it flew towards him at the first touch, slamming a line of fiery momentum along his side when he couldn't control the unexpected motion. He let go and hit the ground on his rump.

My life is a slapstick, not a romance. Alan, thankfully, kept his laughter to a minimum.

Luciano jumped to his feet and dusted off the landing site. *That's right. I'm still plenty strong and graceful.* "Let's go get our Commander."

They crossed the hallway.

"It'll be much easier from this side." Alan popped the panel beside Rhiannon's door, and started messing with these new innards. The green glass mini-saw made a re-appearance, as did "Men of Harlech."

Onward! 'Tis the country needs us / He is bravest, he who leads us.

Luciano tuned out the magic surgery. Rhiannon looked so still, too still, on her cot. The blanket really was velvet, with a thick maroon pile and decoratively fringed edges. It wasn't the sort of thing you gave a normal prisoner, only a Queen-in-Captivity. He wanted her to wake and give him some sign that her beautiful brain remained undamaged. Even if she only ordered him to the pilot house once again, it'd be proof that she'd live to frustrate him another day.

The strong line of her purpling jaw, the romantic mussing of her dark hair, the bruises beneath her eyes— these all combined to make her seem too fragile. He wanted to spirit her away and wrap her in a dozen of those velvet blankets until she was warm and hale and his cherished Rhiannon again, not this doll who destroyed dreams.

"Aha!" Alan's quiet crow interrupted Luciano's contemplation of their Commander. "I've got it. Try her door."

Obligingly, Luciano did, ready this time to use appropriate force. Obligingly, the door opened. "I'll carry her." He headed for the cot. "Can you find the tube thing?"

A stranger's voice answered, "It doesn't matter. You're going back where you belong." Muffled by the textured carpets, the man's approach hadn't been heard by the Hive mates until it was too late.

Alan's shoulders slumped in resignation as he turned around. Under the man's boiled-fish gaze, they left Rhiannon's cell and trudged the few feet back across the hall. There was no point in fighting. No one here could back them up.

191

"And I'll be turning off the failsafes, I think," said the man after he locked them back in. "You'll just have to hope there isn't a real fire."

The man turned and left their cell-side. He entered Rhiannon's cage and checked on the unconscious Queen with a doctor's manner. He listened to her breath, her pulse, her heart. If he hadn't been looking after her health, Luciano would have thrown him off of her.

Dear Lord, I can't even do that much.

He sank back down onto his cot, no further along than he was an hour ago. On the other cot, Alan lay straight, staring at the wall behind the two remaining glass vases.

The engineer's eyes were blank, creepily empty of intelligence or ambition. Luciano already missed the singing.

Cymru cannot yield.

CHAPTER TWENTY-TWO

Make Anybody Like You in 50 Easy Lessons

Rhiannon woke to a dry mouth and a shouting match. Whatever she was lying on had an uncomfortable flimsiness, at odds with the warm blanket across her shoulders. The latter might have been made of the softest animal fur.

"Don't you dare ignore me! *Gesú* give me strength."

The argument petered out there momentarily since the second participant apparently refused to participate. That did not keep the first from resuming when silence reigned for too long.

"As God is my witness, if you don't get up and get working, I'll... I'll... I'll tell Commander Ceridwen."

Well, that was worth opening her eyes for, even though she was pretty sure it was going to hurt. She pried open crusted lids, only to squint against the pervading light. More prepared, she tried again, this time achieving full—if washed-out—range of vision. She tried to say, "Hey, you two," but the words caught on the sand drying out her tongue.

That just meant she'd have to try harder. A good Queen or Commander could lead her Hive regardless of physical ailments. Out of love. The university syllabus she'd read explained that Queens and Commanders were not allowed to take sick days. Sick Queens showed up or they lost their Devotees.

Right, then. She was an actual Queen and Commander, not just a student. She could do this. Steeling herself against the disorientation and headache she knew were coming, she tried to sit up. She didn't get far. A few inches. She fell back into a supine position. Her unstable cot didn't provide the necessary resistance for difficult actions like *getting out of bed*.

She could see the boys across the hall from her now through double bar obstructions. Alan and Luciano continued to argue. Well, Luciano cajoled and Alan ignored him. She'd have to do something about that. As soon as she could get their attention.

She levered up on a shaking elbow, but didn't get the chance to talk with her Hive members. Stalking down the hallway in her direction was the man who'd met them at the airlock. Gravel Man. He'd seemed in charge so far. Maybe she could get a few answers out of him, even talk him into letting her Hive go. Really, this had all been a misunderstanding. She'd tell him about that mouse

Llewellyn, and then he'd send her on her way. Right?

Gravel Man checked on her boys first, glaring at them as if they were escape risks. Then he turned his focus to her. "Tell me where she is."

That sounded unfortunately like the questioning that had gotten her beaten and tossed in this jail cell. What were the next consequences of having *no idea* what he was talking about? Might as well ask.

"You know that I have no idea what you're talking about, right? Some guy just told us to give you the case. Which we did. So you should let us go." Oh great. Now she was babbling. Just what they needed.

Gravel Man growled, a sound also unfortunately familiar. "You were supposed to deliver my *Queen*. Where is she?"

Whoa. Why was she surprised that Llewellyn had screwed them over like this? The politician had black-mailed her Hive, given them illegal drugs, and sent them to a clandestine meeting. Yet, somehow, she had a hard time believing him party to Queen-napping. That was just... beyond the realm of possibility. Who would be monstrous enough to separate a Queen from her Hive?

Not the time to worry about this, Rhi.

Now was the time to remember everything she'd read about human interaction. She needed to get Gravel Man calm, to make him see her as an ally. *Rhiannon and Gravel Man vs. the Universe.* She'd prefer to research more, but she didn't have the luxury. So, let's start with sympathy.

"What's she like, your Queen?" She kept her voice

quiet and curious. No threats here. Friendly conversation about a topic dear to your heart, Gravel Man. She doubted he'd notice her gambit's transparency. Not if the feral madness that afflicted those Devoted who had lost a Queen already had him in its grip.

He didn't take the bait. Just grunted and said, "You should know, complicit bitch." The crow's feet next to his eyes gave him a mean look when he narrowed his lids. As though the cracks in his face mirrored the cracks in his Queen-deprived mind. But then he hunched over and took a deferential step back from her cage bars. "Apologies." He actually sounded apologetic, like he'd gone too far. But too far for a kid her age, or too far for a respected Queen?

She wished she really did have the natural people skills which she'd claimed on the Test. Or the right sort of clever Perceiver-ship.

Again, it wasn't the time. Not the time for wishing. Not the time for regrets. This was the time for suborning the kidnappers. Time for displaying the charismatic leadership she'd read about. And a real Perceiver-level Analyst could play any role she knew the basics for. Rhiannon knew the theory behind making people do what you wanted. She'd been studying for weeks.

If at first *sympathy* didn't succeed, try again with something else. Tactic two: Get him off balance. She'd outdo him in aggression. "Those fuckers!" Aggressive idiots did a lot of swearing, right? "How dare they steal your Queen?"

196

Whoever *they* were.

Gravel Man snapped out of his meek posture, vibrating with anger. "Yes." He bit out the word and retook a step towards her like a predator. "How dare you? Only a few days, you said. We just need to ask a few questions, you said."

No, no, no. He'd gotten off track again. He wasn't supposed to keep accusing her. He was supposed to charge after the real villains and leave her innocent Hive alone.

"Hey now." She raised her hands to ward off his attack. "I'd never separate anyone from their Queen." Which raised the question, where was Gavin? He'd come with her whereas Luciano had not. Perhaps, wherever Gavin was, he had Victor and Gwyn with him?

Gravel Man slammed an open palm against her cage's bars. She scrambled backwards from the violence and the noise, tripping over her blanket. Though she needn't have bothered. The bars that held her in also kept him out. There had to be something extra in them because he bounced away, clutching his hand to his heart.

It took her a moment to realize that he was mumbling, more to his sore soul than to her. She crept forward on the floor, hoping to avoid his notice, but to get close enough to hear him.

"It's only for a few days. Only a few days. Been more than a few days. Need to find Marla. Find where they moved her." The poor man rocked himself and his injury back and forth. He'd held up remarkably well in the wake of these obscene circumstances forcing him to survive without his Queen and to take on her role in keeping her Hive together. But how much longer could he last? Was he stable enough to realize he needed to let Rhiannon go before it was too late for all of them?

"Ah, look, ah, Gravel Man," she started without knowing what to say. All she knew was that she wanted to comfort him, to take on his pain for a little while, to give him some respite. And to get him to let her *out.*

Thankfully he wasn't listening, otherwise he might've taken umbrage to his moniker. Also thankfully—because she was failing like a water tank that went brackish blue instead of clear when the Hydrolyze tablets dropped in— two men approached. One was the white-haired gentleman she remembered from her arrival. She rubbed her sore jaw.

The other was young, much younger than the rest she'd seen. He called out "Mister Bristow!"

Gravel Man straightened. Bristow's dry eyes sharpened and met hers. Neither of them looked away until the newcomers closed. Rhiannon wished she could figure out what he was thinking.

Her main jailer nodded to her. *A worthy adversary, perhaps? Or the satisfaction of an interrogation well done?*

"Gentlemen," he said to his compatriots. "I leave these three in your capable hands."

Guards. Great.

"Hey!" she yelled to his retreating back. "Where are the rest of my Hive?" He wouldn't keep her in suspense. He knew the pain of separation intimately.

He didn't turn around or pause. "They're safe on this ship. Worry about yourself."

Well, that was helpful. Ish.

"So," she said to the new guards. "What are you guys up to today?"

They ignored her completely. Professionals to the hilt. She'd have to find some other way to crack this pair.

***

She didn't think of another way to crack them before they traded shifts with a third man. Having guards put a damper on any conversations she might have held with Luciano and Alan.

Her Devoted made faces at each other and checked her for obvious injuries across the distance. But they formulated no escape plans, discussed no personal issues. She didn't like Alan's listless look, though he'd perked up a bit and watched her cell like a delicate experiment.

At the next shift change, the white-haired gent and the young man showed up to relieve the evening guard. A third relief guard also came on scene—his grey hair started at the back of his head and fell in a steely braid down to his shoulder blades. *Braiding! I should do my hair like that, in case of weightlessness.*

Luciano and Alan were still asleep. The youngest guard rolled his eyes at the three older ones. "Mister Bristow put me on morning duty," he said. "And seriously. Do we need three people for this?" He jerked a thumb at the sleeping prisoners.

The steely braided guy frowned, his white moustache making the expression extra deep. "Mister Bristow put *me* on morning duty."

The eldest gent pointed out, "The sleeping ones are dangerous."

Dangerous? That was the first she'd heard of it. Across the hall, Luciano wasn't sleeping anymore. He'd woken in time to hear that evaluation and was kicking Alan awake too.

"Dangerous?" The youngest echoed Rhiannon's thoughts. "Them?"

Rhiannon supposed she should have felt offended on her Hive's behalf. After all, Luciano was definitely the physically strongest with his solid workout routines and muscular chest. And Alan was perilously smart compared to most of the universe. Still, they *looked* as innocent and sleepy as lazing lambs.

Steely Braid narrowed his eyes and put his hands on his hips. "I'm on duty, and you can't make me stop." So resolved, he took up a stance in front of her bars. She admired his hair's tight practicality even more from this perspective.

The evening guard hadn't left yet, leaning with studied casualness against the wall next to her cell. Clearly the unfortunate ship needed better entertainment.

This was her chance to try and get some of the crew on her side. They had to be hurting for discipline and leadership if their Queen was missing. Plus, it sounded like Mr. Bristow was starting to lose his administrative prowess. Hadn't she seen millions of films about Hives falling into disordered madness in the wake of a Queen's death? Maybe she could endear herself by filling the void and arbitrating the dispute? On the one hand, it might make the guards more efficient. On the other hand, where was she going to go if she escaped? Especially if she couldn't find the others.

She could solve their problem with just a *little* more information.

"Excuse me?" Their heads swiveled towards her, and she watched the braid mostly not move. She didn't meet anyone's eyes, her head submissively bowed for now. *Get them used to me.* "I couldn't help overhearing, and maybe... that is... do you have anyone on duty for the afternoon?"

The vicious white-haired gent snorted. "Like we'd tell you our plans."

She shrugged, keeping her posture deferential. "It's just we haven't had three guards before. Maybe this was a mistake and one or two of you are supposed to look after us later. You wouldn't want any gaps, right?" She had to assume a very small crew for this to work. That seemed likely from what she'd seen outside her cell so far. Did they even have enough Devoted to watch over her split Hive effectively?

Steely Braid looked up and down the corridor. "I didn't hear about anyone else taking afternoon."

The night guard shrugged. "I'm back on tonight. You can figure this out on your own." He left.

Good. She hadn't mentioned asking Mr. Bristow for clarification. Neither had anyone else.

Steely Braid looked after his departing comrade and cocked his head. Coming to a decision, he punched the youngest one in the shoulder. "You've got this under control, kid." He held out his hand and gestured, *after you.* "C'mon, Mac. Let's grab some coffee."

Then there was one. Of course they took her advice. They wanted a woman to make their lives easier. They were programmed for it.

Rhiannon offered to the remaining guard, "You probably don't want to tell us when your shifts start and stop. You don't want to be predictable to prisoners."

The youngster—at least ten years older than she—grinned at her, pacified by her logic and willingness to be a good prisoner. "Thanks." He turned his back, watching the hallway vigilantly.

She had a bit of his trust, but she hadn't turned him to her cause yet. She needed to widen the crack of fellow-feeling she'd started in his heart. The right tactic here: friendship. She could do this. Small talk. She sat on the floor right in front of the bars. Making herself small, harmless, very casual. "My name's Rhiannon. Or Commander Ceridwen, I guess."

"Hey. I'm Jon," he said. "Can I call you Kerry?"

Ugh, no. Shorter and sharper than the overlong *Ceridwen*, it felt too cutesy. Plus, she couldn't tell how he was spelling it. Well, she'd let it go. She wanted him to see her as cute, childlike.

"Of course," she said. "I like your boots, by the way." They were standard black boots, calf-height with a small heel. But small talk was about making connections, giving compliments.

"Thanks," he said.

Wow. This was painful. She supposed the next thing to say was *Lovely weather we're having*, but did that work on a spaceship?

Jon saved her from making such a pathetic comment by offering it himself. "What's the weather like back home? It's been a long time, but I remember cherry blossom trees in summer."

And so it went. She told him about the silver maple leaves at the park and about the Beltane "fires" at the spacedock. He told her about training to be a pilot. They commiserated over mice in the grain stores, not that she really knew anything about that, but she filed away the information for later. She encouraged him to call up his love interest from university, even though they both knew his own Queen Marla had to approve first. She asked him all about his utterly uninteresting dating history.

By the time Steely Braid came to relieve Jon for the afternoon, they were both sitting on the floor. Jon lumbered to his feet and mumbled a blushing "Bye, Kerry" in defiance of Steely Braid's disapproval.

INTERLUDE 2

Beneath the Capital

For the third time in as many weeks, Queen Olivia sojourned to the capital city to answer questions about that troublemaking backbench MP, Llewellyn. The former Captain Ceridwen wished she'd never heard of him nor helped book his passage on her former ship. She could only hope that the new Commander hadn't had as much trouble on his account. Last week, the questions had concerned the fact that he'd gone off-grid, untraceable somewhere between the *Cauldron* and the English station.

Bloody English. Probably their fault. Whatever the problem is.

Now they let her know that they'd tracked him down again, not that anyone appeared to be doing anything about the supposed breach of *something*. Was it a breach of technology, state secrets, propriety? No one felt like informing her. They just asked question after question, always the same. *Have you remembered anything new since our initial interview? Would you tell us again exactly what you said that first day? When did you last see Llewellyn?* Et cetera, et cetera.

This trip into the city, she hadn't bothered to bring her Devoted along. By now, the meetings had a routine feel to them, and official buildings were safe enough. Let her men busy themselves with new hobbies and soak up sunshine on a crisp day beneath the shade of the silver maples.

Although her first official debriefing with Jay Rogers had taken place in the Senedd building itself, her subsequent audiences had all been off-site with a variety of government employees. This time she approached an old building, only one story above-ground with white paint peeling off the poured plastic. In her day, it had been part of the governmental complex. These days, it was an old, barely-maintained structure where minor functionaries held pointless meetings. Such functionaries *never* had important meetings; they only thought they did.

"Your ladyship," a guard at the door greeted her. "If you'll come this way."

She'd never been met by a guard before. Of course, she'd never come without her Devoted before. Etiquette might require an escort since her own was absent? At least the man was polite.

She followed him down three flights of stairs, but balked at the fourth. She'd only ever been on the ground and first-underground floors.

"Wherever are we going, guardsman?"

His unhelpful reply: "If you'll please follow me."

She stopped. "No, I will not. You will explain or we will go no further." She'd come here of her own good nature, willing to do her part for society's safety. But she drew the line at mindless obedience. That was for children and the young Devoted, not for Queens who remembered when the paint on this building was fresh.

Seeing that she wasn't about to budge, the guard grasped her elbow. *He laid hands on her inviolate person.*

"Please, your ladyship. Don't make me hurt you."

The very idea! And yet he was touching her. He dared to direct her this way. Would he be willing to hurt her in truth? He might.

Shoulders back, head held high with her white hair curling around her ears, she swallowed her disquiet and allowed him to lead her down, down, down. Twelve floors underground, she saw and smelled sour evidence of life. Women languished behind metal bars, many wearing the gowns and crowns that marked them as Queens of the realm. Some looked scragglier than others, hems torn or hair tangled. Food bowls of the kind one might give to a dog sat on some cells' floors. Prison-style latrines offered no privacy.

"What is the meaning of this?" she asked, cold and in control. She wouldn't struggle.

Off to the side, a young Queen's black hair pieced from her braided crown. Her bare arms were scratched and browned with dried blood. Her cries echoed through the room.

"I can't feel them. Where are they? What have you done with my Devoted? *I can't feel them!*"

The guard pulled open the door to an empty cell. "Your ladyship."

He gestured Queen Olivia inside. She saw no recourse but to enter the room with as much dignity as she could muster. She sat on a hard cot, the only furniture available, and crossed her hands in her lap. Prim. Proper. She inclined her head to the guard, dismissing him.

He locked her in before taking his leave.

The woman in the next cell, not wearing a crown or any finery, introduced herself. "I'm Marla, Queen-Captain Llyr of *Llyr's Llambo*. I'd ask what you're in for"—she grinned with wry misery—"but no one's in for anything."

Who would imprison Queens of the realm? She'd been duped. The official interviews had been an excuse to get her into confinement, not a way to acquire information about a missing politician. *Foolish, Olivia.* But she couldn't truly condemn herself. She'd had no reason to believe her home planet was an enemy battleground.

"I'm Queen Olivia Jones," she replied to her neighbor. "A pleasure to meet you." Although it wasn't, not if she had to be here.

The woman nodded as though she'd heard Olivia's thoughts. Abruptly, she folded in half and vomited bile. Olivia did her best not to react to the noise or the stench.

Olivia would have liked to soothe her through the sickness. But the other Queen had fallen to her knees above the grated drain in her cell's center. Too far for compassionate touch. Olivia raised her voice. "Shall I call a guard? Have them bring a doctor?"

Marla pushed back to sit on her heels. She spat into the drain. "Don't eat the food. It's drugged."

Our captors caused such sickness on purpose!

Olivia felt despair rising like her neighbor's gorge. Her Hive didn't know she'd been taken prisoner, would not realize for some time, and certainly wouldn't look for her here. She could only hope they'd be all right without her, that they wouldn't descend into madness before she could escape.

Llewellyn. She choked on guilt. Would the new Commander Ceridwen be likewise penalized for his presence in her life?

CHAPTER TWENTY-THREE

With My Body

Victor had spent five days curled up in the warm red shadows of his cell, shared with Gwyn and Gavin. Often Gwyn rested her head against his shoulder, thigh, or stomach while Gavin kept to his own side of the large room. Four times a day, someone dropped three food trays into the comfortable cage. Other than that, their captors let them alone. The food-giver, a man with grey plaited hair, called them things like *harmless* and *spare* and *not worth watching over.*

Victor wondered how the others were doing, if they were even together or rent asunder yet again. Did they merit a guard? Possibly. The Queen-Commander, pilot, and resident genius had so much more to offer than he did. So much more to hurt them for.

At some point, he knew, their captors would give up on this gentle treatment. Wasn't it an evil-doer's requirement to harm innocent victims? Still, for now all was right. He had his health and his love. He had his best friend. His freedom could wait.

He had nothing to do but cuddle in the dark nest he'd made, cocooned in silken privacy panels. He'd refused Gavin's attempts to continue his quarterstaff training with poles they'd found. What was the point?

Gwyn sighed against his neck. He felt her melancholy all along his side where she pressed against him. "I always thought we'd have more time. Maybe kids and a farm."

He wished he could give her those things. "All I have is this velvet captivity, but I'm glad to share it with you."

They wallowed in woe together, content as sheep in a small field. Daringly, her hand snuck under his tunic to lay flat against his stomach. Just resting there. Warm connection and unspoken promise of further touches in some alternate future. The touching could go no further, of course. Not with Gavin in the room.

Gwyn said in a soft voice, "We could have some goats and cows, running around over wide open acres."

Victor played along, adding to her dream. "They'd all line up to be milked at ten of the morning. We'd have two barn cats named Cat-Gwyn and Gwyneth."

She kneaded her nails into him, imitating the imaginary cats. "Would you call me Lois?"

That surprised him, but not enough to make him move from his comfortable place in order to look at her. Her parents had given her one name, but—

210

"But I've always called you Gwyn."

She sighed again, air puffing against his Adam's apple. "It's not my name. Not really." She'd gone by *Gwyn* for longer than Victor had known her. Every year on the first day of school, all the teachers called *Lois* and got corrected. Corrected by her, by him, by someone else. "Rhi nicknamed me for my white hair. I think we were ten."

And wasn't that statement an open emotional well? *The gods all hate me, don't you?* "Don't you like it?"

He hoped that was the right sort of answer. He'd known something was going on between Gwyn—*Lois?*—and her best friend, but he tried not to think about their potential troubles. He tried not to think about his girlfriend and his Queen in the same sentence at all.

He wanted to keep them separate in his mind. Wanted to compartmentalize his lover's love far away from his Hive life. Not like his father. His father who abandoned his non-Hive family whenever his Queen or his Hive mates called.

Gods. Victor didn't even have a true Hive life to call him away. He'd never even said the words. Never pledged his Devotion.

Gwyn wrenched herself out of his arms, but stayed close enough that he could smell the starchy morning gruel on her breath. Her intense eyes turned almost green. "It's not my name."

His beloved was unhappy. His Queen was unlinked by the bonds of Devotion. He didn't know how to fix any of this.

"Shh." He pulled her into an embrace, this time to console rather than to cuddle. "Your name is Lois." He called on his godly patron to let her understand his seriousness. "And may Lleu smite any who tell you otherwise."

With a *mewl*, she curled more deeply into his embrace. He was pretty sure that indicated acceptance and contentment.

A loud stomping shook their nest. Victor leaned to the side and peeked through the screens to see Gavin pounding his boot heel against the floor.

"What is wrong with you two? Our friends are missing, our lives are at stake, and you coo and canoodle in the dark?" He loosed an impressive, theatrical roar. Then he watched Victor and waited for a reaction.

And waited. And watched. And waited.

Fine. I'll say something.

"Just leave us alone, Gav. Let us have our final days in peace." As for the rest of their Hive, unseen since incarceration day and maybe dead, he couldn't worry about them if he didn't think about them.

Gavin paced. His flamboyant green sleeves flapped with furious force. "Final days? My final days aren't coming for a long time. Do you hear me?" He raised a fist as though railing against gods, nature, any onlookers, Victor's preconceptions, whatever he needed to declare *enemy*. It wouldn't do him any good, though, not after five days. Gavin should join them in the calm and the shadows, enjoying the peaceful certainty their captors provided.

But that wasn't Gavin. He wouldn't stop until he was dead.

As Victor watched, his friend moved to the room's center, standing on a sunny yellow carpet in the only lamp's halo. His face turned alien, a strange grimace throwing it all out of proportion. Urgency started in his eyes. He bobbed his red-blond head.

The urgency mounted when he clutched long, bony fingers to his throat. Gavin's large, blue eyes opened impossibly wider, and his mouth stretched to match. He made retching noises. Nothing came out.

His desperate hands slid further down, now tearing his outer shirt's buttons, then the next layer and the next, until he reached the layer protecting stomach-skin from air. He clutched that last bastion, balling the material in front, stretching it too tight in the back.

Victor couldn't move. Could only witness.

Gavin fell to hands and knees in a rectangle, still retching loudly, emptily. He sucked in great wheezes and worked his mouth around unintelligible words. He fell to his side still in a rectangular shape, then stretched out. He convulsed inward again, fingers scrabbling from neck to belly to cover the top of his head.

He went still. His body didn't heave. He made no noises.

Gods. I said nothing would happen unless he died, and now he has died. Gods.

Victor didn't move. Couldn't move. Couldn't get closer to his friend and witness the gory, bitter truth.

213

Gwyn—*Lois*—wrenched herself from the shadows and dropped to her knees at Gavin's side. She yelled to their captors, "Help him! Help!"

But no one came running. No alarms sounded.

When she turned their friend to lay him flat, Victor ordered, "Get back." His voice was tight and high. "It might be contagious."

The dead body wrapped steady fingers around Lois's wrist, halting her quest for a pulse. "Dear lady." He jackknifed to his feet. "I'm perfectly all right. And we can conclude that no one is watching us."

Now Victor did stand and leave his warm corner. In two steps he crossed the room and laid his friend back on the floor with a single punch. "You poison sucker!"

Gavin rolled fluidly back up to standing, brushing off Victor's rage.

"Good, you're up. Let's get to work." His shirts in disarray, Gavin looked like a child playing dress up, not the victim pounding for entrance to Annwyn only moments before.

Lois giggled. Victor whirled on her. *Think I'm funny do you? Think we should all be clever escape-artists like Gavin?* But the words died and muzzled his mouth with their carcasses.

Her giggle turned to two, then three, then high-pitched laughter. It went on and on. Too high, too strong. She gasped for air while her sides fluttered. The agonizing sound bounced inexorably on his ear drums. She laughed and laughed. Tears squeezed from her eyes.

"Shh." He tried to gentle her, push her back into the comforting shadows and their little nest, but she would not be moved.

In minutes or hours, she calmed, her muscles unable to support hysteria. She relaxed against him, her forehead hot and slick against his throat.

Gavin made a *hrrum* noise to get their attention. They both turned to look at him. He'd moved outside his bright spotlight to stand next to the door. "While our hosts have been ignoring that lovely performance, I've been working on something better."

With a flourish, the Handsman slid their cell door open. "Ladies first." He made a sweeping bow in Gwyn's direction. She winced when she giggled, but gamely let go of Victor's supporting arms and strode through the door.

Gavin followed right behind her until Victor's two best friends in all the galaxy were standing in the bright hallway. Funny. When they'd started in this Hive, Gavin had been the outsider, not really a part of Dyfed's culture and not knowing anyone other than Victor. Now, Gavin had an important job, and had made Gwyn—*Lois*—smile when Victor couldn't.

Gavin had his Queen's love.

What did *Victor* have? He had a choice between his girlfriend and his Queen. He had no purpose or position in a Hive that already had a better CreaTech and a better Handsman. He had no life at all. He was that picturesque train station where "no one left and no one came" in the poem.

Well, not anymore. If he was the empty train station, then he would build an engine from scratch and ride it into the greater world. If Gavin could be a good Devoted, so could Victor. If Lois could change her name, her life-identity, then so could he.

He could be the poet instead of the poem. The poet who had joined a war for the poetry.

If nothing else, he could join them in the corridor and see how the future played out. He certainly didn't have one in here.

Before the others had the chance to notice his hesitation, Victor strode past them. "Let's find the rest, shall we?" A man surrounded by friends couldn't be an empty train station.

Gavin hopped to catch up. He pointed down another corridor, this one with even deeper carpets than in the holding cells. "I hunted the ship's circuits for our comrades before we liberated ourselves. There ought to be another holding pen down that way."

But things were very different in the corridor where the remaining three Hive members languished. For one thing, they were split into two cells, not one. For another, Rhiannon's cell sported a guard. Even if he was a lax one who was too busy chatting with their incarcerated Queen to notice that the young men behind him were orchestrating their own escape with crosswired panels galore.

"Hey," Gavin said, the ultimate in casual.

The sound got the guard's attention. Victor moved to loom over the young man. All he had to do was *not slouch* and he towered over this guy. "You don't want to try me."

Gavin popped the panel outside Alan and Luciano's cell, starting there instead of making Victor move his current hostage. The moment his door opened, Luciano thanked them for the rescue.

Alan, though, was a different story. "Oh, yes, it's so very difficult to open a prison door from the *outside*." He didn't sound impressed. "I'll have you know I've broken out of this cell three times now. Twice requiring effort and intelligence."

Gavin didn't look at all dismayed by Alan's sneer. In fact, he slung a companionable arm around his Hive mate's shoulders, magnanimous and friendly in the face of disdain. "Let's hope it sticks this time, yeah?"

Alan scratched at his left eyebrow, ducking his head to do it. "Yeah. Thanks."

They both smiled, and Victor knew that Gavin had become a real Hive member. No question now that he'd gone from outsider to valued friend. All while Victor himself had taken steps in the other direction. Well, no more. He was a member of this Hive too, gods witness it, a founding member.

Here lay his chance to prove his usefulness and Devotion: breaking out the Queen. "Well." He clenched his teeth when he spoke to the guard. The grinding made a disturbing grating sound. "Do I have to do this myself?"

The intimidated guard didn't have the chance to answer. Rhiannon spoke instead.

"Jon." Her voice was soft, more compassionate than

he'd ever heard her with anyone, even Gwyn. "You know that we're not a threat. You know that we've been duped as much as you. You know you'll be doing the right thing to let us go."

For the barest of moments, no one moved. But the Queen-starved guard didn't stand a chance. Somehow, Rhiannon had known exactly what to say and do. She'd managed to get inside the hostile man's brain and change him into a friend, a partially Devoted one even. He gave in to the inevitable and opened Rhiannon's cell door himself. "The ship-to-ship shuttles are that way." He pointed. "They've reeled the tube in by now."

She stood resplendent inside her former confines, days of dirt and sweat doing nothing to diminish her. The shortest person in the hallway, she had the greatest presence.

Jon stepped backwards, out of her space, and she favored him with a gentle smile. She crossed the distance and pressed a closed-mouth kiss to his cheek. In strong tones, no longer laced with compassion or humility, she suggested, "You should pull the alarm yourself and cover your ass."

Victor would swear that everyone in that hallway loved her a little more after that. For caring about a man in her thrall, for commanding instead of bending or breaking.

A blaring siren broke the admiring quiet. Wails slammed against ears. Red lights flashed warning. A gravelly voice came over the speakers. "Alert. Alert. Our prisoners have escaped and are possibly armed. Recapture at once. Deadly use of force is authorized. Alert. Alert."

He'd heard sirens like this a few days before. *That must've been another of Alan's escape attempts.* At the time, he hadn't had any idea what was going on. *These guys are way more efficient than we are.*

"Run for it," someone said.

Whoever said it, it was good advice. The whole Hive pelted down the corridor that Jon had pointed out. *This shuttle better be straight ahead.* Because they were passing junction after junction and not taking a single one.

Two shots rang out, loud *bang*s that made every sound swim through lead cotton. He saw a dent in the wall where a bullet had lodged in the Kevlar padding behind the metal plates. Maybe they should have taken a junction.

The Hive skidded to a stop. Ahead, a tall man with reddish hair brandished a small pistol. *So small to make so much noise.*

It looked to Victor like the man was moving in winter, achingly slowly and hampered by cold and coat. The gun came up again, and Victor knew what he had to do.

He pushed past the two—three?—Hive mates, forcing his way to Rhiannon's side and beyond. Much taller than his Queen, he made a better target. He wrapped her up in his arms, covering her body completely with his own.

Time sped up again.

Another *bang*. The sound coincided with a burn in his chest, like eating too much hot food so fast that you can't breathe and your body can't cool off and everything has to stop but life keeps moving.

"Huh," he said, surprised. Then, "Sorry" because his weight was draped over Rhiannon and bearing her to the ground. He couldn't hear his own voice above the buzz in his ears and the pounding in his chest.

This. This was his place, where he belonged. Between his Queen and danger. Not in the engineroom or making kiss-love with his girlfriend. Between his Queen and danger.

Gods, I'm such an idiot. Rhiannon wasn't even technically his Queen.

"My sword and my service," he rasped out. And when had he gotten on his back on the ground? His shoulders in Rhiannon's lap, his Devotion made private by a hair curtain. Her face was streaked with crimson blood. Was she bleeding?

He continued, though he could barely hear his own voice over the ringing in his ears, "My body and my blood."

He heard Gwyn—*Lois, sorry*—screaming, but he couldn't deal with that right now. He had to make this right. Had to prove his Devotion. "My agency and my anima. These all belong to you, so I swear."

Salt water fell on his cheeks, but he didn't need to stay awake to clear the tears away. Didn't even have to hear her acceptance.

What he did hear was Jon's muted shouting. "They're just kids!" His voice cracked on the last word. *He must have followed us.*

Feather-light fingertips brushed sweat-coated hair away from Victor's temples. He opened his eyes and read his Queen's lips. He knew the words to watch for. She didn't disappoint. "I accept your sword and service. Your body and blood are mine to direct. Your agency and anima are my agency and anima, now and forever more. Call on me in times of trouble, as I will call on you, but always you will be my first defense."

Her first defense, her last Devoted. Devoted in blood.

CHAPTER TWENTY-FOUR

Promises Fulfilled

Rhiannon held Victor in her arms. *He looks ten years old with his face like this* warred with *He took a bullet for me.*

"Help me turn him over," she ordered no one in particular. They needed to put pressure on the entry wound in his back, or else he'd bleed out. That was the way it worked, right?

Jon was at her side, babbling, though she could barely hear past the ringing in her ears. "Marla was our doctor too, you see." He slid Victor's far arm over his shoulder, not turning him as she'd requested, but dragging the unconscious man to his feet. "But if we get him to Medical, I'm sure we can find something."

Alan edged Jon out of the way, pulling Victor into his arms and carrying her newest Devoted with unexpected tenderness. Her Hive and Marla's moved as a unit, converging around Victor. As though his blood had bound all of them with its touch.

Except for one man. One bystander. One authority figure with a gravelly voice and all the real power. "No." He still held the pistol at chest height, pointed in their direction, stock supported with two hands.

Gwyn started screaming again, but Rhiannon couldn't make out the words. Something about *your fault* and *you owe us* or maybe *he could be dead!* Rhiannon could only see the hot blood, listen for the killer's terms.

Mr. Bristow didn't falter before Gwyn's emotional attack. "Please be quiet," he shouted. A sensible request made sinister by the weapon in his hand. Rhiannon thought he looked different in violence's wake. Steadier. Not necessarily a good thing when she was on the victim's side of an unwavering pistol. "I want you people off my ship. I'll take you back over myself, but you're not spending any more time here."

With a constraint's addition, Rhiannon's mind started up again. Her deductive paralysis evaporated. She saw the corridor in startling clarity—not just the stained floors and hands, but also the painted walls and the people standing in it. She had a problem to solve. And enough information to work with.

Gwyn voiced a wordless wail. Rhiannon put a quelling hand on her arm before she could harangue the man in control once more. "Leave it, Gwyn. If we really want to save him, we have to go somewhere else."

The distraught response caught her by surprise. "My name's not *Gwyn*!" Gwyn shot back, as though that were the most important thing. She stomped to Alan's side. Ran trembling fingers through Victor's hair. "Don't call me that ever again."

Mr. Bristow ignored the emotional byplay. He finally lowered his weapon, agreeing with Rhiannon's assessment. "Anywhere but here."

True to his word, Mr. Bristow organized Rhiannon's Hive's evacuation. He made his people set up the ship-to-ship bridge again, and he personally rigged a sling for Victor's transport. Once in the suits, no one could talk nor hear anyone else. Rhiannon couldn't help being grateful—both for the quiet and for the lack of chances to anger the Queen-deprived crew again.

Once they'd returned to *Ceridwen's Cauldron*, Brysen Bristow left them with this message before opening the airlock one last time: "We're going to find our Queen. And if I learn that you and yours had anything to do with her abduction, no place will be safe for you ever again." His wild eyes and the pistol strapped to his space suit foreshadowed his madness's return. No one doubted his word. "We're keeping the money as damages."

Then he departed. Just like that, the threat was gone. The ship was hers again. She was home. Safe.

But not. Because home was far away where the silver maples shed their leaves. Where Dad crunched numbers and Mom was buried. Where she'd had a well-planned future. And safe didn't include a boy—a *Devoted man* who belonged to her—fighting for his life.

224

Not home. Not safe. But all hers. And she couldn't relax, lest it all be taken away.

"Luciano," she said. "Take this man to Medical and give him whatever care you can." He was the only one with anything resembling the experience or inclination.

Technically, Gwyn had been running the Band-Aid Box for the trip, but no one had needed it yet. Plus, Gwyn wasn't really capable of more than she had managed so far: helping Luciano to guide the stretcher and babbling encouragement at Victor's still form.

The three sped off. They pushed Victor along without any bumps or juggling.

Time. Victor's was in question, and all the *Cauldron* was on a tight schedule. They had to get out of this area, and get out fast. As soon as the adults got back to their ship, Mr. Bristow could change his mind. Could decide he'd given them enough leeway. Could lose control and rid the galaxy of two Hives at once.

One Hive member taken care of. All the rest to go.

Rhiannon raced to the pilot house down corridors that seemed more empty than before after seeing all the homey decorations on the other ship. "Corner!" she called as she approached one, not caring that everyone she might bump into was elsewhere accounted for.

Up the ladder. She threw herself into the seat, ignoring the myriad switches and buttons, consoles and lights and panels. Jon had told her all about piloting, had been happy to discuss his hobby and his desire to qualify for a full license. She only had to determine her destination and check the vector maps—easy math for a Perceiver-by-nature—before pressing *Go.*

She only had to plug in her destination.

Her destination.

Where would they even go?

Manawyddan as my witness, I want to go home.

Had it really only been five weeks, forty short days since they'd left home?

But there was no home anymore. Queens were being abducted, according to the men of *Llyr's Llambo*. Llewellyn had made it clear that home-baked authorities were dangerous to her Hive. Besides, she'd promised Victor and Gwyn that she'd help them. Gwyn was her best friend. And Victor. Victor had spilled his life to hold on to this chance.

Where can we go instead? She pulled up a map and blocked off sections. Away from Dyfed space. Not going near the *English*. Someplace with a spaceport.

The closest outsystem, non-English dot on her map belonged to a spaceport orbiting an American colony, pushing the boundaries of English territorial claims. *John Wayne Station.* She estimated the distance, the fuel, the air requirements. She checked those estimates against the available stores. Not enough.

She checked a rough measurement for going home against available stores. Not enough.

She checked a rough measurement for going back to the English station, where Llewellyn might still lie in wait to use her Hive again, against available stores.

Not enough.

It didn't matter what destination she picked. They'd never get there alive. She picked the American spaceport.

When she called down to the engine room, Gavin answered. After swallowing a mouthful of Tribute, he told her, "There's no way we can push the engines any faster or more cheaply, Commander. You just can't do it."

She didn't tell him that if he couldn't get her to one spaceport, he couldn't get her to any. No use in sowing panic. She called Alan's room next. What good was having a physics genius if he couldn't be called on in times of dire need?

"Can we do anything to the engines or the ship's weight? Anything to get to this outsystem port?"

Alan's answers were more to her liking. "Well, there's my personal project, my lady. The miniaturized Alcubierre tensor jet."

And he says it's not magic. "The goddess Ceridwen must be looking out for us. Get with Gavin to hook it up. Immediately."

"Ah, ma'am." He only got extra-formal when he had to censor himself out of deference to his Queen. Well, she'd accept that. "It *should* get us there on the fuel, and it *is* tensor fast, but I can't guarantee how long it'll take. And I haven't had a chance to, you know, test it. And—"

She knew what he needed to hear. "I trust you." Whether she did or not, whether it worked or not, Alan's hobby was their only hope. "Get it set up."

CHAPTER TWENTY-FIVE

Deus Ex Engineer

Alan stumbled through the door to the engine room, balancing his miniaturized Alcubierre tensor jet drive in one hand. The drive wouldn't do any good if he dropped it, but it wouldn't do any good in the corridor either.

When this is over, I'll look into voice activating the doors in case of emergency.

Ah, good. Gavin was already there, munching on a Tribute. Gavin was above average in intelligence. Though not in Alan's class, he was capable of helping him hook up the drive. "Good, you're here. We're going to add an outsystem drive."

Gavin loped over and took Alan's baby from his hands.

"Careful!"

With a worryingly casual shrug, Gavin put the delicate machinery down on a table with no respect for its importance. "This ship doesn't have space for an outsystem drive. You can't fit a mature maple in a dwarf-apple plant box."

Alan tilted his head down and scratched at the bridge of his nose, holding back the words he wanted to say: *Let's try this again, idiot.* He pointed to the mass of machinery he'd brought along. "Our illustrious Queen and Commander has ordered us to make that work. It's an experimental tensor jet drive. Don't think you can take credit for it with the Science and Technology Eisteddfod Medal committee. That's my personal project, and you're only getting to see it because Rhiannon commands it."

Gavin wore an obnoxious, indulgent smile, and Alan realized he might have gotten a little off topic. The smile washed away, replaced by a slight opening of the mouth that showed off pearly teeth. "Is she serious?"

Alan thought about calling on deities for help explaining. *Our Queen wants us to set up this thing* was all Gavin needed to know. It was a simple concept. But Gavin deserved a little more respect than that. After all, while Alan had been oh-so-busy hiding in his cabin, too far away from home to cope with strangers and Llewellyn, Gavin had solved the oxygen crisis. And they'd both managed to break out of jail, even if Alan's situation had been much more complicated.

So instead of making his usual show of no confidence, he smiled through bitten cheeks and shook his head. *Oh those silly non-engineers.* "Isn't it always the way? If you need a miracle," he started the old engineroom saying.

Together they finished it: "You call an engineer!"

Alan nodded. "Right. So, let's get to work."

First they diverted all power away from the planetary and in-system drives. They didn't have the man-hours to get everything working in concert. Either they'd fly by tensor jet, or they'd be driftwood.

As he spliced and hooked, Alan found himself humming "Men of Harlech" again. *Foes on every side assailing / Forward press with heart unfailing.* Since his first escape attempt, he'd had it stuck in his head. All his lab partners at university had groused that he sang while he worked, so maybe it wasn't such a strange phenomenon.

He fiddled with the casing to the drive power box, humming away. For a moment, he faltered when he realized the harmony lines weren't only in his head.

The placid sky / Now bright on high. Gavin had joined in from where he was disabling all automatic calls on the shut-down drives. The ship's Handsman sung an enviably warm baritone.

Gavin didn't even notice his pause, just kept singing and clipping. "Finished! What's next, boss?"

Alan felt a pang of nostalgia for the university and all those older students who insisted on leading group projects. If only they could see him now. *See? Plenty of people submit to the wills of those who know better.* This new faith in his knowledge was gratifying. *I got a better Hive than all those morons.*

"Start thinking about fuel," he ordered, attention focused on the operation in front of him. "You probably won't think of anything, but I'll come help you after I finish this part of the installation."

"Aaaactually." Gavin extended the word like a professor giving a student a chance to recant his utterly incorrect answer. *I'm not going to fall for that.* "The *Cauldron* has a fully stocked garden. We could probably mix up some tincture of Bel—"

Alan didn't let him finish. "Yes! Yes. That's perfect." He elbowed the unfortunate Handsman out of the way so that he could reach the communications system and call down to the plant room.

The call wouldn't connect.

Gavin tapped him on the shoulder. "Gwyn's probably not there."

Alan turned to him and raised his eyebrows. *Gwyn had been running the plant room?* "I thought she was doing Medical?"

Gavin reached past him and made a call. "She did both." But no one answered his call either. "If she's not in her room or with the plants, she's probably with Victor in Medical, and I'm not interrupting that scene."

"Can you—?" Alan didn't know the right way to ask. *Is it insulting to assume he knows anything about plants? Or to assume he doesn't?*

Gavin clapped a warm hand to his shoulder. "I'm on it." And he was gone, presumably to the plant room.

Alan firmed his mouth. *I trust Gavin. I can delegate. I am not a control-freak like Doctor Agosin in my mother's Hive.* Besides, he had to get this wired into the rest of the ship before fuel became the constraining factor. Fuel or not, without the drive, they weren't going anywhere.

Cymru fo am byth! / Onward, Men of Harlech.

CHAPTER TWENTY-SIX

Leap of Leadership

Rhiannon spent two hours plotting courses and adjusting air flows.

She wished Gwyn could tell her how the garden might affect the dangerous carbon production *en route,* but the other woman was too busy and distraught. She wished Luciano could check her math, but the young man was busy working at being a doctor. She wished her Mom were here to tell her that everything was going to be all right.

And if wishes were water, we'd drink by the pint.

Hating the necessity, telling herself it was *just in case,* she recorded a message. Full visual, this time, because strangers trusted you more when they could see you. "This is Commander Ceridwen of the Dyfed ship *Ceridwen's Cauldron*. Please help us. If you're seeing this message, we're all unconscious with hypoxia. Please."

She set the message to repeat when the ambient oxygen fell below 15 percent. Then she turned off the alarms. No reason to worry her Hive. If the stars were destined to swallow their final breaths, let them at least go gently.

Beeps and flashes. Alan calling to let her know the drive was ready. Ish.

Alan, who had carried Victor's bloodied body.

No time to hold a Hive meeting. What good would it do anyway? This was the Commander's call.

She turned on the speakers shipwide. "Hold on to anything you don't want to slide. We're about to move."

She cut the connection. It was warning enough.

She programmed her destination and prayed to Ceridwen, to Manawyddan, to any god who might listen.

Welcome to America

Rhiannon lay on a hard, flat surface.

Not the pilot's chair, then. I must've fallen to the floor. She needed to see where she was, get back in the chair, check on their flight path. Her eyelids refused to part, gummed together.

With a trembling arm, she reached up to rub away the muck. Her questing fingers found unforgiving plastic. She was suffocating. It covered her nose. Covered her mouth. Wouldn't let her breathe. She gasped for air. Pulled at the cold killer with enfeebled hands.

Steel bands closed around her chest, pinning her to the frigid counter. *No!*

"It's all right. You're all right. Shh, now."

Her muscles relaxed. Against her will.

Let me out. Let me up. Let me out!

A deep voice over her head said, "When will she be available for questioning, nurse?"

Hospital?

Everything went fuzzy, which was strange. How could the darkness behind closed lids be fuzzy?

***

This time she woke gently. She listened to the nurses' shoes and instrument carts, clacking on shiny-clean floors. She smelled the antibacterial sprays whose sour-sweetness masked stale sweat and sickness. She felt the thin pillows protecting her from the bed beneath.

One set of clacking footsteps came closer. Rhiannon reached out a hand, glad to find the restraints gone.

"Victor?" Her voice croaked and cracked.

The nurse looked like a white and bronze blob to Rhiannon's sleep-crusted eyes. "You survived whatever happened to you, honey."

She thinks I was in a space battle?

"The man who came in with me. Bullet wound?" She forced the words through her parched, already tired throat.

"I'll find out for you." The nurse patted her shoulder. "You rest now."

The nurse took her choice away. Rhiannon slept, whether she wanted to or not.

***

This time a man was arguing at her bedside. "I want her awake now!" he demanded. If he'd graduated to yelling, he must have been making this known for a while.

Rhiannon didn't give his adversary a chance to tell him *no*. She forced her vocal cords to cooperate. "What's happened to my people? There were six of us, including me."

The man gave his enemy one last word. "See?" He turned his attention to Rhiannon. "All five of your people are recovering, including the one with the bullet wound. He should regain full range of motion in another few months of therapy." She appreciated his business-like attitude and willingness to tell her *anything*. "The two who woke before you have been clamoring to visit. Too bad the nurses rule this ward with a heavy-worlder's fist." *Which ones are awake? When can I see them?* "We got your distress call. What happened to you?"

How to answer that? He didn't need to know about Llewellyn's blackmail or being jailed by Queen-deprived unfortunates. "We ran into technical trouble. Had to use the experimental drive."

He nodded. "We noticed your drive. We didn't think anything that advanced was coming out of Dyfed space."

That's my Alan! She gave the man a weak smile, half apology and half pride.

"Well," he said. "We can discuss that later. Right now I want to know, how do you plan to pay your care and docking fees?"

Rhiannon wished the nurse would knock her out again.

She'd studied leadership skills. She'd studied interpersonal relations. She'd studied piloting.

She'd never studied finance.

END BOOK ONE

Bonus Short Story

So Much to Offer
or
Five Times Alan Didn't Devote, and One He Did

Gavin fiddled with his fraying left sleeve after he left Rhiannon's bedside. Visiting hours were over. Not that it mattered. The staff had kept her sedated the whole time. Still, keeping watch over the woman who'd become so important seemed more useful than loitering outside her door.

Ah, a distraction. Alan was in the waiting room, tip-tap-typing at the one interface non-residents were allowed to use. Gavin announced to him, "Alas, our Queen lies in state." Perhaps that declaration was a trifle overdramatic, even for him.

Not that Alan even noticed.

"Hmmm?" The half-listening boy looked up from the console.

Well, at least he acknowledged me. Now seemed as good a time as any to ask a question that had plagued Gavin since they'd met.

"Why'd you join our glorious Hive, anyway? Someone like you, already known to Queens at higher levels. You didn't even know us."

Alan leaned back in his chair, stretched his arms, and popped the joints in them. He shook his shaggy head as if to say *Poor boy, what little you know of the world.* "Oh, friend. Rhiannon's was the best offer I'd ever had, and I got offers before they could technically come to me, before I took the Test. Some Queens..." He trailed off. Smirked. "Allow me to tell you what I call, 'The Tale of the Five Unsuitable Offers'."

Gavin could appreciate the drama in such a title. He balanced his head on his hands on his elbows on his knees, not caring about the voluminous sleeves that slid down to expose his arms.

This tale can't be worse than sitting by myself.

1. THE MOTHER

When Alan told his Mum that he really, truly, for certain planned on doing his university work in physics, she smiled and told him to be well-rounded. By which she meant: take biology courses.

A year later he explained that he'd already received his bachelor's degree and had begun work on his Master's of Mathematics. This didn't stop Mum from suggesting that bioinformatics was a very computational field and that she could use a strong interdisciplinary researcher to balance her new linguist.

At this point Alan realized she meant for him to join her Hive when he finished his degrees. Now he loved his Mum. He did. And he appreciated all her fine Devoted who had taught him to respect science and to live a life of pure Devotion.

But he had no intention of tying himself to Mum forever. That just... ugh, no. He wanted to feel a rush of affection and helpless love when he found his perfect Queen. He didn't want to always be thought of as Mum's baby. Oh, he could visit for a week or two at holidays, but he planned to make his own choices, thank you.

I'm terribly sorry, Mum, but you seem to be trying to take over my life.

Alan stopped sitting in on cognition and computational biology lectures. He told his advisor that he'd switched his M.Phil. thesis to something utterly theoretical, like differential geometry. The stuff they used for tensor jets.

He'd rather choose some old battleaxe Queen than get stuck behind his mother for the rest of his life.

2. THE OLD BATTLEAXE

Another day, another Maths & Physics mixer. Once a month, the head of the department set aside the Physics of Music theatre to bring together the faculty, the yet-to-

Devote department students, and any campus Queens she could rope in. The warm, inviting space had glorious acoustics, a sumptuous burgundy rug, and lofty ceilings painted with old-fashioned settings of famous Queens— like England's Queen Elizabeth I and Egypt's Queen Cleopatra.

Alan detested these mixers.

He'd liked them well enough in his first year, back when he was only thirteen and not serious about finding a Queen, not even able to since he was too young yet to take the Test. But now that he was sixteen and semi-officially categorized as *Devoted*—though only semi-officially because he'd skipped the Test in order to play with fresh lab data; he'd take the Test next year, but everyone already knew what scores he'd get—the parties were painful to his heart and intestines.

The university-age Queens ignored him as *too young*. Not a problem when he'd started his studies, but it rankled when he was only one year younger than the first year Queens. Then again, he wasn't interested in first years. He gravitated towards the Queens working on their graduate degrees, a species with an average age of twenty-three.

Still, they had no right to treat him as worthless because of his age. He had the same university experience they did. He took the same classes and walked the same corridors. He tutored some of them even! And, too, he would grow older in the fullness of time.

But they dismissed him as inferior. When he engaged one in conversation, they were always looking over his shoulder, hunting for an older, more suitable model. What he wouldn't give to have just one Queen pay attention to him at these things. One bloody Queen!

"Excuse me, young man."

Alan turned to see a significantly older woman, at least ninety years old, standing with rod-perfect posture though she had a mostly-finished glass of sherry in her hand. "If I might have a moment of your time?" She gestured expansively with the drink, suggesting that it might not be her first and showing off an unbecoming purple lipstick imprint. If she'd been here as long as he had, she no doubt needed the fortification.

"How can I help you?" Alan had been raised on a diet of *politeness to one's elders* and *looking out for opportunities*. Odds were good that this older lady was the guest of one of the department officials or faculty members. Getting into her good graces could be a way to gain favor with that lot. With a thesis defense coming up, he could use some friendliness.

"I hear that you're a genius without a Hive," she said.

He waited for the rest of her point, but she stopped speaking there.

All right then. "Ah, yes. Well, modesty forbids my commenting on the genius bit, but I am indeed without a Hive. Though I live in hope. I'm young yet." He tried a smile with that last weak quip. He hoped she didn't think he'd meant to imply that she was *old*.

"I'm a Queen."

Again she said nothing further. He supposed *That's nice* was not the correct response in these situations. Bran's beard! He hated these mixers. Now even the old Queens were getting in on the *make Alan's life miserable* act.

She read his incomprehension in his silence and finally made her pitch. "I can use you, young man. My Hive is respected and well-known—you've heard about the latest in high-power lasers, I trust—but we're aging. We could use an influx of new blood, and you seem a sensible enough boy."

She hadn't come right out and asked him to join her, so he wasn't in the terrible position of turning down a powerful Queen. He *had* heard about the laser work and would have been interested in the project, but not at the price of tying himself to the middle-aged, who'd be geriatric when he hit his own stride.

He cast about the room for something, anything, that might require his attention. A professor who wanted a word? A lab partner who wanted to yell at him for moving an experiment? Anything! His eyes darted everywhere, preferring to look at the dark red floor fibers or blonde wood structural beams or wrinkling tablecloth underneath the sherry. Faster and faster his gaze switched, until instead of hunting for escape, the whole room became a blur of colors and running babble. His head throbbed, not helped by the scope-quick movement of his eyes, but he couldn't stop.

A cool hand squeezed his shoulder from behind. A contralto voice, ever so casual, broke through his panicked haze. "Hey there, kiddo. You got a minute?"

Alan didn't care who she was or what she wanted. This woman was his new favorite person. "I'm terribly sorry," he said to the sherry-drinking Queen in front of him, "but this may take a while." He let himself be escorted away by his savior.

She guided him along till they'd reached the other side of the room, far enough away to avoid the older woman. Safely away, the contralto Queen dropped her propelling hand. Alan turned to look at her.

She was taller than he by at least half a foot and had the kind of open expression you expected from puppies, but mixed with a wry humor that said she knew exactly what she'd saved him from. Her mostly blonde hair was streaked with funky pink, and her black tunic had artful slashes all over it that he'd have made fun of if they'd been on anyone else.

She said, "I hope you don't mind," but she didn't sound apologetic nor worried about what he'd think. "You looked like you could use a friend."

He nodded. "Thanks for the help. I wasn't sure how to explain I had no intention of Devoting to her without sounding like a complete jerk." *Without sounding like the Queens who dismiss me*, he wanted to say but didn't.

The softening of her eyes, though, made him think she understood what he meant. But all she said was, "I'm Beka."

"Alan."

They shook hands in silent accord. It was them against the room of judgmental would-be Hives.

3. THE OLDER SISTER

Alan found himself tutoring Beka in maths after that. She was a poetry major with a brilliant turn of phrase when she needed one. Together they bonded over his favorite kind of poetry—silly stories of aliens, intended for children. She didn't judge his love of supposedly children's literature, nor his willingness to overlook terrible scansion.

Instead, they discussed metaphor and rhythm in between Hamiltonian equations and imaginary vectors.

They met up in comfortable places. Sometimes in a dorm lounge, stretching out on lumpy blue couches while music blared and other Queens surreptitiously held hands with potential Devoted during a film. Sometimes in a library, surrounded by musty books and green-shaded lamps that made everything glow like a plant.

He never met any of Beka's Devoted, if she even had any. They didn't talk about Devotion or love or how they planned to live after university. Half the time, Alan forgot she was a Queen and just relaxed in her presence. She laughed at his jokes, appreciating them even when they became more caustic over time. She gave him balance when he was adrift in a sea of loneliness that stripped away his socialization and ability to interact with other people.

Then she got her B.Poe.—the doctoral degree in poetry—and it was time for her to leave the university altogether. He found out in the dorm lounge. She gave him a sisterly hug, soft and sweet and more comfortable than the scratchy material they sat on, and invited him to her graduation ceremony.

For a brief moment, he considered begging her to stay. Asking to leave with her. The first words were at the tip of his mind. *My sword and my service, my body and my blood, my agency and my anima.* But he kept them all wrapped up in equations and affection. They weren't Queen and Devoted. They never had been. They were friends and allies against the mixers.

"Of course I'll come," he said.

After the ceremony, he never saw her again.

4. THE TOWNIE

When Alan's Test day came, he didn't report to any of the approved locations. Already in his first year of graduate study, he had better things to do that day. Namely, getting in his lab results after four weeks of waiting on an experiment to finish. He had no intention of wasting those first, discovery-laden hours with an activity whose outcome was certain.

He marked his status to sick and had his advisor, Professor Cantor, sign him up to take the Test the following year.

The evening of Test day, though, was a different matter. Students worldwide held outlandish parties. He

247

couldn't bear to attend any of the campus events; they'd fill up with dismissive collegiate Queens and jockeying Devotion-hopefuls. Perhaps he should have stayed in the lab with his new data, but he'd worked the day away and felt ready for some fun.

So he went into town.

University students weren't allowed to attend townie parties. With all university males being Devoted, they couldn't afford to accidentally meet and fall for some non-Queen woman. With all the university females being Queens, well... that set must be protected from reality at all costs until they had more experience.

It logically followed that townie parties were the most popular.

Alan's lab partner, in a bizarre fit of generosity or maybe relief that Alan remained officially un-Devotable, shared his invitation to a large dance mob well outside the hallowed halls of academe. The pair of them dressed in their most daringly tight-fit tunics and hit the town, all smiles.

The party itself was in a brutal concrete building with exposed rebar and a strange lack of cobwebbing. The high ceilings were reminiscent of a hangar, but Alan rather thought the interior design was just for show. The place reeked of perfume and sweat-activated aftershave. His ears rang with heavy beats and screeching fiddles.

In mere moments, Alan lost his lab partner to the humid teenage crowd. That was fine with him. He hadn't really intended to hang out with the older student any-way. They didn't even like each other.

Across three cliques and a keg, Alan caught the eye of a pretty townie girl about his age. She had Asian heritage in her smoky eyes, played up by a thick line of kohl that didn't allow for lid color. Shimmering black hair waterfalled straight from the crown of her head to the nipped waist of her bold, red tunic.

His heart sped to the time of the musical booms. His palms heated and moistened to match the air. When she walked toward him, he hesitated for a mere moment, trapped by expectations and the knowledge that he was going to fuck this up.

And then he remembered that he wasn't Alan, potential Devoted, to this crowd. Here, he was a townie. Just a guy out looking to party, who would never see any of these people again after today. Except for his lab partner, who he expected to see two days from now at 11 a.m.

She stopped in front of him, head tilted to see him better.

"Hello," she said.

At least, he thought she said that. The music was so loud, he really had no idea. He yelled back, "Heya," and accompanied that word with a wave. Preliminaries over, he felt awkward. But he wasn't going to let that keep him down. He could be suave tonight and go back to too young and too smart tomorrow. No pressure at a townie party, remember?

He gave up on talking and pulled the beautiful young woman into the vigorously dancing throng scant feet away. She laughed, showing off perfect teeth and a wide smile, fetchingly turned half away from him as if in modesty.

She wound her arms around his shoulders in order to press even closer, which seemed a bit odd with fast music, but Alan didn't intend to deny her. She was so close now, he could taste the chemicals in her hair from strands that accidentally caught in his mouth. His heart synched with hers, separated only by skin and rib cage. When she breathed out, he breathed in. The music faded away, wrapped up in woolen mufflers, letting him concentrate all his senses on the visceral beauty in his embrace.

He didn't know how long they'd been dancing before she ran fingertips down his arm, from bicep to inner elbow to wrist, to pointer-fingernail. His body tingled in the wake of her touch, the internal shiver radiating inward from his covered skin, up through his limb, to lodge in his now-stuttering heart.

She grasped his hand firmly, a sudden counterpoint to the tease of moments before, and tugged him to a dark alcove. He didn't pay any attention to the partiers they passed or the exact coordinates of their new location. He only knew that fewer intruding presences surrounded them, that it was quieter in this new space, and that the townie woman looked even more mysterious and darkly alluring with half her face in artistic shadow. She couldn't have picked better lighting for herself if she'd planned it.

She positioned herself against a wall and grasped the nape of Alan's neck with her free hand. For a moment, he worried about the sweat he could feel moving under her caress. But she didn't seem bothered, so he let himself go with the flow. And when she pulled him down to rub their lips together, he went along gladly.

He sucked in a breath, heartbeat picking up tempo. The fleeting kiss filled him with a jangling anticipation for more. And why wait? He leaned down again, this time the initiator, to reach the contact he craved. His lips parted to feel her on as much surface area as possible.

His hands clutched her waist of their own volition. She disengaged her mouth, and he tried to chase her down, but she put him off by brushing their cheeks together. The softness of her skin against his half-stubble sent shocking percussion through his nerves. Her warm breath enveloped his earlobe as she whispered, "Alan, dear one. Let's seal our affection upstairs."

His name never sounded so right. He imagined the shape of her face, forming the syllables with excruciating deliberation. He longed to hear it again.

My name! He'd never told her his name. They'd never had a chance for introductions. University parties could be like that—a lot of kissing without knowing anyone's name.

He could only think of two reasons for her to know who he was. One: Mother had sent someone to keep an eye on them. Two: She was a Queen from the university trying to entrap him! (He dismissed the possible number three: someone playing tricks. You saw that sort of thing in books, but not in real life.)

He threw her away from him like lab data that had been contaminated by a biased researcher. "What do you want?" he yelled, loud enough to be heard at this distance. Under the light of suspicion, her dark eyes looked more nefarious than sensual, her make-up more cakey than sexy.

She lunged toward him, arms extended, and he thought she was trying to regain the close embrace they'd shared only moments before. That, or strangle him. Either way, he danced backwards from her reach.

She didn't try a second time. Instead she planted her feet shoulder-width apart and put one hand on a cocked hip, head titled down for maximum derisive impact when she gave him an exasperated *look*.

"You like me, right?" she said. "I'm interesting and caught your eye. You're half in love with me already. So just Devote already, and we can get on with our lives."

Half in love with you, is it? I don't even know you. In trying to show off her people-smarts, she'd proven just how useless she was. He'd been interested in dancing, maybe more, with a pretty townie, not in signing his life away to some Queen he didn't know anything about. When he Devoted, he'd have a relationship with her already, or at least a healthy respect for her intellect. This girl was nothing to him, just one of the manipulative masses.

"No thanks," he said. No reason not to be polite.

He left her there, shocked and annoyed, in the corridor. He stepped outside the brutal building into the sharp, cold night air with its picking rain and hired a skimmer. He still had lab data to go through back at the university.

5. THE PERFECT QUEEN

The night after Alan finally took the Test, his department held another mixer. This one was smaller, just for Queens and Devoted in the department, no attendees from the community. The organizer had chosen to use the Senior Common Room, a cozy spot with a fireplace and studded leather couches and space for thirty people.

The size of the gathering made this the quietest and most intimate departmental mixer that Alan had ever been to. Plus, more people talked with him than ever. Professor Cantor had stopped in to chat about his second thesis. One of Beka's closer male friends had told him that she was piloting a spaceship and writing children's literature these days. His lab partner was ignoring him.

Maybe these mixers aren't so bad.

Beka's friend came his way again, chatting with a Queen only one year older than Alan, a second year at the university. The Queen glided along, gracefully aware of her own body, only slightly shorter than Alan but much more elegant. Her tasteful silver circlet looked like infinity symbols chasing each other through her wheat-colored hair.

Beka's man introduced him and walked away with a wink. Alan rolled his eyes in response. Queens never went for him at these things, and he didn't know this new woman at all. He didn't mind so much these days, though.

After meeting Beka, he'd acquired new perspective. If he didn't Devote now, he'd Devote later. He could tell people he'd Devoted to Lady Science, until such a time as he found the perfect Queen.

He wasn't sure a perfect Queen existed, but his work at the university and under Professor Cantor promised to be fulfilling—and *funded*—for some time.

The Queen's petal-pink lips quirked at the side. "The young man across the room only has awful things to say about you." She gestured at Alan's lab partner. *Great, now no one will want to talk to me at all.* "His ire made you sound so interesting."

"He does have a well-formed mind," Alan agreed, tone and words in direct opposition.

The Queen laughed, wide mouthed and unselfconscious. Alan was charmed.

They spent the next few hours discussing her course of study, the same as his as an undergrad, and the more *interesting* professors they'd both met over the years.

Alan had never spent so many hours with a Queen before, aside from Beka, who didn't count. He wondered if this was what a *good date* was like for the non-Devoted, less-brilliant classes. He wanted to do it again.

"What are your plans for tomorrow?" he asked, when the scout started ostentatiously *not* shooing people out of the room, simply cleaning around them. "If it's not too forward..." He lost useful words for a moment, unsure of how to say *what if I like you?* He lamely attempted, "I think we might suit and would like to find out." It sounded horribly old fashioned and stilted, but at least it got its point across.

She raised a hand to her mouth and widened her hazel eyes. Affectation or true surprise, it didn't matter. She didn't even have to speak. She'd made her disinterest in him as anything more than a conversation partner clearer than the dome over the Old Capital.

Without a word he turned on his boot heel and walked away. He headed straight for the door, then to his dorm room, taking no detours, not looking at the night-blooming flowers or vomiting post-revelers.

Safe in his room, he huddled under his midnight blue duvet, letting the warm cotton wrap him in reassurance. He couldn't be disappointed. He barely knew the girl. He had Lady Science and funding and friends.

He wasn't crying. His tear ducts were just helping him to cool his overheated face.

6. THE CHEAT

Alan didn't think much of the young woman—probably his physical age—who entered the lab without warning. He'd never seen her there before, and Professor Cantor *abandoned* him on her arrival, which made her presence extremely suspect. Clearly she wasn't here to work. He'd bet she had gotten lost or was the flighty type who couldn't be bothered to stick with a scientific discipline.

Then she asked for him by name. That was a terrible sign. It meant she'd be littering his lab for ages. He could do without any more Queens trying to use him or be his friend.

She held out a hand for him to shake. "Rhiannon, soon to be Queen-Commander Ceridwen."

He turned his back on her and made sure she could see he'd started playing a match-3 game. *You're not even worth working while I ignore you; you're only worth a mindless amusement.*

"No thanks. Send Professor Cantor back in if you see him. I'm not interested in whatever you want me to build for you or in becoming your prodigal slave. I've met plenty of Queen-Commanders. I'm not desperate."

That should send her running. He'd be prickly and impossible to work with. He'd make a terrible Devoted for a young thing like her, rolling over her desires in a second.

"I bet you have," she said. "I bet the older Queens and Commanders wanted to control you, for your own benefit of course."

He thought of the old battleaxe Queen who wanted fresh blood in her Hive. That one had interesting projects but she hadn't wanted him for *him*.

The girl, Rhiannon, continued. "I bet the younger Queens don't treat you like a real person. They make fun of you for being a kid."

His fists clenched in anger. Yes, anger at all those unseeing Queens who didn't realize what a good thing they had with him. They weren't clenched with sadness or a need to rub his eyes. Certainly not.

On closer inspection, she didn't look all that silly or flighty, just a bit young in her too-big tunic. He could appreciate that she'd come all this way to track him down, that she'd bothered to think about what he needed and what his life was like. Most Queens he met thought about themselves and their needs, nothing more.

Rhiannon was still talking. Now he gave her his full attention. ""I bet you honestly want to find a Queen of your own. One who trusts you. One who treats you like a full member of the Hive. One who understands that you'll be just as interested in your research as you will be in her. One who doesn't expect you to dance attendance on her, but who does provide structure for your days and opportunity to mingle with other brilliant people. One who will make sure those other people take you seriously as well. One who likes you for you, not for your skills or the prestige you bring her."

Something was off with this young Queen. Yes, he'd been pleased that she'd given thought to his situation and desires, but she seemed so sure of herself and her analysis. He narrowed his eyes, hunting for more clues and details about this near-stranger who'd shown up in his computer lab.

She didn't wear a crown of any kind, like most newly minted Queens did, though she was certainly of the young-and-freshly-made variety. She had an unassuming presence, not palpably taking up all the space around her, like most Queens he met.

"You're not a Queen-Commander at all, are you? You're a Perceiver!" He'd never heard of such a thing, never thought of it. On reflection, any Perceiver *should* be able to game the system, regardless of whether they wanted to. Oh, this was delicious.

She smirked at him, superior and inviting him to join her in the smarter-than-the-world joke all at once. "That's not what the Test says."

She might turn out to be another useless Queen. She might be terrible at leading a Hive. He might hate all of her other Devoted, who were surely her little sixth form friends. But she was smart and unconventional. He couldn't help but like her moxie.

They traded a few more volleys of conversational proof-of-cleverness, but Alan had already decided. With exaggerated grace, just a tiny eyeful of mockery to show that he knew this Devotion was real but also somewhat melodramatic, he fell to the floor in front of her.

"I pledge you my Devotion. My life and my hands are yours for a year and a day," he swore. "May we choose never to part."

"And that," Alan finished, "is why I joined your Hive instead of staying at the University."

Gavin eased back in his chair, shaking out his arms and bouncing his legs to improve the circulation. "Those other Queens, I simply can't believe." He couldn't figure out how to form the sentence he wanted. Usually, he'd find an apt quotation in a moment like this, but somehow, just, no.

Alan got up and walked over to pat Gavin condescendingly on the head. Gavin would remember to be annoyed later. Maybe. "That's why we Devoted get to choose the Queen we want. Someone out there wants those other sorts, but not us."

We really are a lot alike. Gavin forgot all about being mad at Alan. *I'm glad we're here together, and with Rhiannon.* Their Queen would get better soon, and they'd all forge ahead. Together.

END "SO MUCH TO OFFER"

About the Author

Janine A. Southard writes speculative fiction and videogame dialogue from her home in Seattle, WA. She sings with a Celtic band and is working on the next book in the Hive Queen universe. She's also been known to read aloud to her cat.

The cat appreciates all of these things. Maybe.

Interact Online

Visit her on the Web: www.janinesouthard.com

Interact on Twitter: www.twitter.com/jani_s

www.ingramcontent.com/pod-product-compliance
Lightning Source LLC
Chambersburg PA
CBHW050923120626
46552CB00001B/20